I0630712

THE GOOD DAUGHTER

Laura DiNunno

Copyright © 2020 Laura DiNunno
The Good Daughter was originally published as Daddy's Girl under the name L.E. Falcone in 2016 by Red Collar Books.
All rights reserved. This book or any portion thereof may not be reproduced or used in any manner whatsoever without the express written permission of the publisher except for the use of brief quotations in a book review.

Names: DiNunno, Laura, author.
Title: The Good Daughter / Laura DiNunno
Revised edition
Summary: A young girl seeks revenge with deadly consequences.

Library of Congress Control Number: 2020905002
Subjects: Psychological—Fiction. | Thrillers—Fiction. | Cross-country running—Fiction. | High school students—Fiction. | Female friendships—Fiction. | Friendship—Fiction. | Children, abuse of—Fiction. | Girls, crimes against—Fiction.
Published in the United States of America by Red Collar Books.

This is a work of fiction. Names, characters, businesses, places, events and incidents are either the products of the author's imagination or used in a fictitious manner. Any resemblance to actual persons, living or dead, or actual events is purely coincidental.

One

Dad warned me to stay away from girls like Eden Rhodes. On the first day of cross-country practice, I hung back and let her set the pace so I could keep an eye on her. She was a good six inches shorter than me, but her thighs were thick with muscle. She glanced over her shoulder and caught me watching her, but I played it off like I was pacing the runner in front of her.

For someone so short and athletic her stride was smooth, almost graceful. She ran track last year, setting a new record for the 100-meter—the best in the tri-county region. And here she was running cross-country. When we were near the end of the run, I blew right past her.

"It's the first day of practice, Christa. Don't push it," Coach Paul said, looking sort of impressed and sort of irritated with me.

"I know," I said, finding my breath. The final sprint winded me, but I tried to hide it in case Eden was watching.

"Cool down and hit the showers," Coach Paul shouted. "Good work today."

As I walked, I rubbed my quads and shook my legs out, searching for Eden while trying to look like I wasn't. Soon, I felt someone beside me, someone short with messy brown hair. She was out of breath, almost wheezing, and soaked with sweat. I fought the urge to study her mannerisms.

"This is tougher than I thought it would be," she said, gasping for air.

At the end of junior year, Eden got caught hooking up with a guy under the bleachers. Some jock on the football team recorded it on his phone and passed it around to the other guys at school.

"Giving up already?"

"Don't get excited. I just don't like losing." She eyed me then jutted her chin in the direction of the school. "Race you to the locker room?"

"You must like being humiliated."

After the bleacher incident, the slut shaming haunted Eden all summer—whispers behind her back at the mall, guys coming to the restaurant where she worked, hoping to hook up with her. It never got her down, though. She shrugged it off, and by the beginning of senior year, it was like it had never happened.

Eden dug the shoe of her push-off leg into the ground. I crouched down, preparing to sprint.

"Go!"

Eden took off like a cat that had gotten its tail stepped on, but it didn't take much effort to catch up with her. With my long legs, she had to take double the strides to even keep up with me. I wasn't going to let her win no matter what. I owned cross-country. The sooner she understood that the better.

"I win." I threw my arms in the air and pranced about. *I always win.*

"Dammit." Eden leaned on her knees to catch her breath.

I copied her moves as if it would somehow transform me into her.

"Next time I'll beat you." She put her hands on her hips and walked in circles. "I'm so out of shape."

"You'll get there." I reached to pat her on the shoulder just as Janel Fowler rushed out the locker room door and shoved me out of the way. "Watch it."

Janel ignored me and focused on Eden. "Something came up. An emergency with my little brother, so I can't drop you off."

"Oh no. I hope it's nothing serious."

"Not sure, yet, but I have to go like five minutes ago."

"I can take her home." The words came out of my mouth with a little too much enthusiasm, but I had to take this chance to talk with Eden. With the chaos of school and practice, she wouldn't listen to me, and we weren't exactly friends, so I had to find a way to be alone with her. "It's no problem."

Janel flicked her eyebrows. "Christa Pierce doing something nice for someone? Color me shocked."

"Don't you have an emergency to go to?"

"God, you two." Eden threw her head back and growled. "You're worse than the women on those reality shows."

"I gotta go." Janel shot me a nasty look and stormed off.

"Are you sure it's not a problem?" Eden smiled, weakly. "I think we live in opposite directions."

"It's no big deal."

"If it's no big deal, then okay." Eden shrugged and headed to the locker room.

"You want to come over and study?"

"Today? Well, I—"

"If you're busy then—"

"I mean, sure." She turned toward her open locker and dug inside her backpack. "It'll be fun." She threw a towel over her shoulder and disappeared into the steam of the showers.

This was perfect. My dad was going to hate her. I could almost see it. Eden and I would be studying at the dining room table and he'd walk in after work, take one look at her, and make that disapproving face I knew so well. He wouldn't cause a scene right then, but later he'd talk shit on her. It was easy to do.

Her curly brown hair always looked like she had just rolled out of bed. She must have bought her clothes at the thrift store. The few times I stood near her, I caught a whiff of cheap perfume and stale cigarette smoke. Dad gagged at the smell of smoke on someone's clothes. I sat near her table at lunch whenever I could. She was usually loud, snorted when she laughed, and

4

burped like a sloppy drunk. Everyone at the table thought it was oh so cute. She could probably spit on the sidewalk and no one would even care. But my father would.

On the drive to my house, Eden talked nonstop about her new boyfriend, Kyle Jenkins—the one she got caught with under the bleachers. Sometimes she got explicit with the details. It was a little gross to listen to, but I kind of enjoyed it. Not in a perverted way. It was just that no one ever talked like that around me, and here the coolest girl in the whole school was sitting in *my* car, sharing *her* secrets with *me*. Unfortunately, I couldn't squeeze a word in about what I wanted to talk about—the whole reason for offering her a ride home.

"So, it looks like I'll have a date for prom," Eden said. "I have to start saving money for the dress now, though. You need to find a date. Most of the senior class will be there. We have to leave this dump on a high note."

"The prom isn't my thing."

Out of the corner of my eye, I could see Eden studying me. "I get that vibe. But you should go, anyway. At least try."

"We'll see. Anyway, here we are."

With her mouth hanging open, Eden gawked at my house. "I heard you had money, but I didn't know you were this rich."

A lot of people assumed I was a spoiled rich kid because of my dad's position at Milford University. If we had a lot of money, I didn't know it. Dad kept a tight grip on the finances, and I got a small allowance of about $100 a week.

"I guess that was a dumb thing to say."

"It's all right. My dad won't be home for a few more hours so you can look around if you want. Just don't touch anything."

Eden jerked her head back, smirking. "Are you serious?"

I nodded and pretended not to notice when she raised her eyebrows while mumbling, "ooookay," under her breath.

I took her in through the garage into the mudroom, because, God forbid, I got any dirt on the floor. "Leave your shoes by the door. Rachel gets bitchy if I don't take my shoes off after school. She thinks schools are full of germs."

"Who's Rachel?"

"My stepmom. Dad married her after my mom ran off with some guy when I was two." I made sure to emphasize the important words, so it would pique her interest.

"That's sad. My dad took off when I was seven."

Good. She took the bait. I had heard this story of Eden's many times, mostly while eavesdropping in the halls at school or sitting in class or near her at lunch. She treated each mention of her father as if it were the first

6

time out of her mouth, adding more to the story each time. It came up at least once a week.

"I didn't know your mom took off when you were a baby. It sucks, doesn't it?"

"I never knew her, so it doesn't bother me. I don't even know what she looks like."

"You're lucky, then." She grew quiet, looking sad enough to cry. "Wow. This is so weird."

"What is?"

"I never thought I'd have anything in common with someone like you."

"Someone like me? What does that mean?"

"Well, you're rich." Eden tugged at the zipper tassel on her backpack. "And I'm not."

"I don't know what to say to that." I grabbed two bottles of water from the fridge and passed one off to her.

"I'll shut up. I'm the queen of saying dumb shit."

"Princess?" My dad's voice boomed from upstairs.

I fumbled with the bottle, spilling water down the front of me. "Dad? I didn't know you were home." I looked at Eden, scrambled for the bottle cap on the floor, and grabbed a towel to dry my shirt. "Crap."

Before I could get myself together, my father was in the kitchen, straightening his shirt and tie. "Hello," he said to Eden. "Are you a school friend of my daughter's?"

"This is Eden Rhodes." I managed to get the words out of my mouth in one complete sentence, my jaw and throat automatically clenching when he was around. No matter what he was saying, I stiffened up at the sound of his voice. "She runs cross-country with me."

"Nice to meet you." My father greeted everyone the same way, whether it was an old lady or a kid: his hand was out, palm facing downward, ready to shake. His loud voice carried the weight of promises if only you'd vote for him.

Eden took his hand and smiled. "And you." She didn't cower in his presence or act like she should bend her knee and bow her head, which was how I felt most of the time. Why couldn't I be more like her?

"I didn't know you were home," I said, my voice cracking. "I didn't see your car anywhere."

"Christa." My dad's syrupy voice filled the kitchen. He put his arm around me, his hand squeezing the back of my neck, letting me know I better behave myself. "You can have friends over any time you want, especially Eden Rhodes."

That wasn't the rule, and we both knew it.

"We're going to study," Eden said, unapologetically.

"That's all right. I'm glad you're here. I see she did something right in offering you a beverage."

A door slammed shut upstairs. My father's eyes followed the noise, but the smile never left his face.

"Is this place haunted?" Eden giggled and winked at me.

"I must've left the window open in my room and a breeze caught the door."

"I was kidding."

Dad's face grew pink. My stomach flipped with excitement at this reaction. He doesn't allow others to embarrass him. I liked that Eden didn't give a shit about his fragile ego.

"Well." He clapped his hands together and rubbed them vigorously. "It's getting late. Maybe you should take Eden home. It was nice meeting you. Don't be a stranger." My father stood in the doorway like a guard, barring our entrance to the rest of the house.

Eden slung her backpack on her shoulder and glanced from my father to me. "Okay. It was nice meeting you, too." I could tell by the sound of her voice she was confused and offended by the polite suggestion that she leave.

Out in the car, I apologized, even though I was satisfied with what had happened. I invited someone over without asking permission first—something which was never allowed—and the person just happened to be the type Dad didn't want his daughter associating with, and someone who cracked a joke at his expense. "I didn't know he was home. Honest."

"Where's his car?"

"Who knows?" I did, actually. It was still at the university. As I drove along the street, just a block away from the house, I spotted the car of the woman he had been sleeping with. He'd walk home from his office on campus to meet her there by cutting through the soccer field and a small grove of trees. He thought no one knew, especially Rachel, but everyone did.

"That's okay. I need to get home to make dinner for my mom anyway."

"Maybe we can do it another time," I said.

"If you want."

"It'll be fun."

"Big fun." Eden flipped through the radio stations, mindlessly. "I'm sure you get this a lot, but you're the spitting image of him. Like twins."

"You're right. I do get that a lot."

"I mean, it's freaky scary."

"How do you think I feel?" Long legs, broad shoulders, same blonde hair. If my hair wasn't long, no one could tell us apart from behind. This was the perfect segue. "I don't know what my mother looks like, so I can't tell if there is any of her in me."

Eden stared out the window as I drove along the streets of the subdivision, craning her neck as we rode past some of the prettier houses in the neighborhood. "Do you ever wonder what she's doing and where she is?"

"I shouldn't, especially after what she did to me. I mean, who leaves a toddler behind to chase after a man?"

To be honest, I wondered about her a lot lately. Something happened to me over the summer. Something clicked, something changed. I was tired of not knowing the truth, tired of life at home, tired of everything, really. I wanted to know where my mother was, what she was doing, what she was like. And if I could get back at Dad in the process all the better.

10

"Do you think about your dad?" I asked.

"All the time."

There was no better time than that moment. "We should search for our parents. Together."

"No. Way."

I had a feeling she'd say that, but I had hoped I dropped enough hints to warm her up to the idea. "Why not?"

She let out a sharp breath. "Because if my dad wanted me in his life, I would be."

"Maybe he has a good explanation for what he did. Did you ever think of that?"

"Like what?"

"I don't know. I always thought my father was lying to me about why my mother left."

"Why would he lie to you?"

"Just a hunch."

"And, so, you think my mother is lying to me?" She waved her hands around wildly, like she was getting pissed off.

"No, but there are always two sides. You know your dad, so only you can tell if what your mother told you is true."

"I suppose. I was only seven when he left."

"At least you knew him. I mean, it's hard to miss someone I don't even remember, but…" I took a deep breath. "I still wonder about her."

Maybe I needed to hear myself say it out loud. Somehow putting those words out there made it real, and there I was trying to convince another person to help me search for her. Sure, I could do it on my own, but Eden had something I didn't have: confidence. She didn't give a shit about much of anything, least of all getting in trouble. The whole bleacher incident proved to me that she was stronger than most of us at school, and I wanted some of that, too.

"What are you thinking?" I said, breaking the silence.

"You said your father lied to you. How do you know?"

Because he lies a lot, was what I wanted to say, but I settled for something simpler, something that wouldn't derail the direction of the conversation. "I refuse to believe my mother would leave her two-year-old when she could've taken me with her."

"Maybe she couldn't."

I didn't want to hear or believe that. "I was a baby. What do babies do wrong? Except for the pooping thing, not much."

She let out a long sigh. "You know what? I change my mind."

I nearly drove off the side of the road when I heard the words come out of her mouth. "Do you mean it?"

She pressed her lips together and nodded, fighting back tears.

My chest swirled with energy. I couldn't remember the last time I felt this happy. I was about to turn seventeen and wanted to know what really happened to make my mother leave.

"What if my father doesn't want to see me at all?"

"You have a right to know."

I pulled into the driveway of Eden's rundown, double-wide trailer. She stared out the window and laughed. "After seeing your house, mine looks like a shack."

"I'm not here to judge." But it was hard not to. The white vinyl siding was now a dingy grey, with splotches of green algae near the overgrown shrubs used to hide the cinderblock foundation. The front screen door had strips of silver duct-tape holding the screen to the door frame. I bet her house smelled like an ashtray or sour milk or soup. Places like that always made me think of a can of soup.

"Listen," I said, "let's keep this idea between the two of us. Do not mention—"

"Do you think I'm nuts? My mother would be pissed if she found out I was looking for him." She took a deep breath. "There's no one else I can talk to. No one ever takes me seriously or maybe they just don't want to hear about it anymore. You're the first person at school to ever act interested." Eden wiped her cheeks with her hand. "Now that I know about your mom, I know you get it."

I tried so hard not to smile. She took the bait like a hungry fish.

"How do we do this?" she said, solemnly.

"We'll go online in the computer lab and see what we can find, I guess."

"Perfect. We can keep it at school so no one finds out."

"Not a word to anyone. Promise?"
"I promise."

Two

When my father is in a good mood, I try not to push my luck. I don't usually ask for special favors or do anything that might draw attention to myself. It's a relief to have him act like a decent human being, and I always take it when I can get it.

It was last minute, but I wanted to invite Eden to go out to dinner with us on my birthday. Dad tolerated Eden at his house, but he probably thought it was a one-time thing. Well, it wasn't. We had been sitting together at lunch, in class, and challenged each other on our runs ever since that day. He couldn't control who I hung out with forever. And I really could have used a dose of Eden's *fuck it!* attitude to help me get through the evening.

I had asked Rachel to ask Dad if it would be okay because Rachel was better at getting him to agree to things than I was. He'd listen to her before he'd ever listen to me. I waited outside his office, my ear close enough to the door without actually touching it. I only heard mumbles. At least there wasn't any shouting. That was a good sign.

Dad came out of his office first and went straight upstairs, not evening looking at me as he walked past. Rachel was right behind him and headed for the kitchen.

"What did he say?"

"He wants it to be us, just family," Rachel said.

And family to my father meant those who were living under this roof. Even if I had been friends with Eden my entire life, he would still say no. I made it sound like it was Eden's idea and not mine. "She was hoping she could come. She practically got on her knees and begged me."

"The two of you can do your own thing later."

"I suppose, but she'll be disappointed."

"It's only one night, Christa." She slammed a cupboard door shut. "I have more important things to worry about than upsetting your little friend." Rachel might have called me out on my bullshit, but she never raised her voice to me. Dad's latest fling must have been getting to her. She never took her anger out on him, though.

Rachel was the only mother I knew, but we weren't close at all. I could never go to her with a problem or open up to her, unless it was about my father. That was the only time we bonded, but afterward she pretended like we never had a heart-to-heart. To be honest, I never felt completely comfortable confiding in her. She was always cold and kept together, even when my father was nowhere in sight. The only time I ever saw her relax was when she had friends over for drinks, and that was years ago.

16

When I was a little girl, and he went out of town, my father paid me to listen in on her conversations. She thought I was playing on the floor with my dolls, but I only pretended to dress them up in their pretty party clothes. What I was really doing was playing spy. He paid me a dollar to sit and listen so I could report back and tell him what she had said. I never told my father everything she said—sometimes I'd make things up—but I took the money and hid it in my jewelry box. By the age of thirteen, I had fifty bucks.

"He wants you to wear a dress tonight." Rachel gave me a disapproving look.

"It's rainy and cold. Can't I wear my good pants?"

"We're all dressing up, so go pull something out of the closet and get ready. Put some makeup on and take your hair out of a ponytail for a change. No more whining."

Defeated, I started to walk away but stopped. "Is someone important going to be there?"

Rachel's eyes darted back and forth. "Not that I'm aware of. Why?"

"He's making us dress up? For dinner?"

"Gerard's has a dress code. It's your birthday. He said he wants you to feel special."

"He did?" I felt myself smile. I felt myself allowing my face to smile. Was Dad chilling out? His mistress must have been something else.

After a painfully silent, painfully long drive to the restaurant, a waiter kindly pushed the chair in behind me. The table was situated right in the middle of the restaurant where everyone could see us. My father pinned on his plastic smile, stirred up his syrupy voice, and gesticulated in his usual look-at-me-I'm-important sort of way. He smiled and waved at strangers at other tables like he was their best friend. Despite his happy mood, which was always a welcome change even if it was an act, he hadn't even wished me happy birthday. Hell, he barely noticed me, not once commenting on the dress I picked out or the smoky eye I managed to create. So much for feeling special.

I buried my face in the menu, studying the main courses. Salmon, grilled in a honey and ginger glaze over spinach and brown rice sounded perfect, and since it was my birthday Dad wouldn't mind. But just as I was about to order the salmon, my father interrupted me.

"We'll all have the roast chicken breast, steamed carrots…"

Rachel and I exchanged glances. I didn't want chicken. I wanted salmon. I despised carrots. It was *my* birthday. A quick glimpse of the menu showed the chicken was at least ten dollars less than the salmon.

As we ate our salads, my father slid a powder-blue, rectangular box with a big blue ribbon on it across the table. "Open it." His voice was louder than it needed to be in such a cozy setting. "It's your birthday." He smiled and surveyed the room to see if anyone was paying attention, which they were.

I wanted to crawl under the table. I didn't want to open it while everyone was staring.

My father put the napkin to his mouth and grumbled. "Open it."

I tugged at the fancy bow and opened the box. It was a bracelet. White gold with embossed roses on the plate. "It's beautiful. Thank you, Dad, Rachel."

"Read the inscription on the back."

I turned it over and squinted to see three little words: For My Princess. I swallowed hard and forced a smile. "Aw, that's so sweet. Thank you again, but you didn't—"

"Stanley Murkowski," my father said, jumping from his chair. Oh, look, it was the county commissioner and his plastic trophy wife. So that was why we came to this particular restaurant and sat at this particular table. He didn't want me to dress up because it was my birthday or because there was some dress code. Someone was going to be at this restaurant tonight. Someone important. Someone who could help my father further his career at the university or help him with his political aspirations. This had nothing to do with me and everything to do with him. I knew it was too good to be true.

"Dr. Pierce, nice to see you again."

The two men greeted each other like old fraternity brothers in some secret society. I expected to see the secret handshake any second.

"Stanley, this is my lovely wife, Rachel."

Rachel extended her hand, followed by the commissioner gesturing a kiss on the back of it. "Nice to meet you," Rachel said, practically drooling at meeting someone important.

"Likewise," Stanley said.

"And this is my beautiful birthday girl, Christa."

I didn't dare extend my hand so I waved and smiled. "Hello."

"Happy birthday, young lady," Stanley said, winking.

I thanked him, wanting to hide. Everyone in the restaurant was watching us.

"She's seventeen," my father added.

Stanley smiled and nodded. "My youngest just turned seventeen. Soon they'll be off to college." He winked at my father and the two huddled closer together, speaking softly.

It didn't take long for everyone in the restaurant to go back to their business, and as they did, I let out a long exhale.

Rachel reached across the table, motioning for the bracelet. "Let me help you put it on."

"Don't bother." I tossed it in the box, fitting the lid back into place.

"I think you should put it on." Rachel had an edge to her voice. The message was clear. I had to be the perfect little birthday girl and do what I was told.

Knowing Dad couldn't hear me, I said: "I don't understand why he still calls me Princess. He knows I hate it."

"Hate it or not, put it on." Rachel gave me a pleading look. "Now."

"I'll wear it later."

My father immediately stopped talking to the commissioner and shot me an acid look. He heard me. My body stiffened.

"Let's get together for lunch soon, Stan." Dad waited until the man walked away before taking his seat calmly. His smile remained steady as he scanned the room, but his hands were active with nervous energy. He tapped his fingers on the table like a woodpecker working a tree. Once the commissioner was seated at his table and distracted by the server reading the specials, he turned his attention to me sharply. "Give it to me," he said under his breath.

"What?" I squeezed my knees together. "But you—"

"Your stepmother and I searched everywhere for that particular bracelet. We had it engraved especially for you, and this is how you treat us? Ungrateful bitch. You don't deserve it. Hand it over."

Rachel buttered a slice of bread from the basket in front of her like none of this was happening. I slid the box across the table, not meeting Dad's gaze.

"I'll have to keep it, I guess. Unless the jeweler can find another father who calls his daughter Princess. Thanks for ruining my evening and for embarrassing me in front of the commissioner. And don't bother apologizing."

I stared down at the plate of iceberg lettuce with its carrot shavings and nasty looking cucumber slices, clenching my jaw to keep my teeth from chattering. It didn't matter how much confidence and courage I leeched from Eden or that I was getting older or how rebellious I felt, I was still afraid of him. Slowly, I released the breath I held and coaxed myself to take another. My father and Rachel started talking and carrying on as if I wasn't there.

Over the years, I had mastered the art of eating while the muscles in my neck were so tense I could barely swallow. That evening, I swallowed exactly thirty times—thirty times I felt I was going to choke on that dry chicken breast.

The ride home wasn't any better. If they'd left me behind in the restaurant, they never would have noticed. I was that invisible. It could be a good thing. I was going to get the silent treatment, at the very least. I wasn't going to get grounded, though. Never did. When I did something wrong, I was punished in other ways. Unless my shirt flew up, no one could see the bruises.

Three

After the humiliating experience at my birthday dinner, I had a new sense of urgency to search for my mom. Between the time I suggested it and the Bracelet Incident, Eden must have changed her mind about searching for her father at least a dozen times. I talked her off that ledge each time until she accepted it was just as much her idea as it was mine.

Computers hummed in the cramped, overheated lab. Students were face-deep, messaging on their social media platform of choice or watching the latest viral video. Some actually worked on homework assignments. I slipped in unnoticed, scanning the room. Dad wasn't around, but that didn't stop me from looking over my shoulder. Between deep breaths, I had to remind myself I wasn't doing anything wrong.

Eden sat at one of the computers in the back corner. Usually, overly hormonal couples sat there and slurped on each other's tongues because it was private. I slid in the chair next to her. We studied each other. Her pale face and curious eyes told me she was as nervous as I was.

"How do we do this?" she whispered.

"I guess like any other search."

"Well, duh. I mean there are a lot of guys named Randy Rhodes in the world."

"Where does he live?"

She didn't answer, only worried the string on her hoodie.

"What'll I do if I find him and he doesn't want anything to do with me?"

I had the same thought. What if Dad wasn't lying and Mom really abandoned me for some guy?

"I can't give up now, though. It'll hurt like a bitch, but I need to know."

I pretended she successfully convinced me. "You're right."

While Eden did her thing, I typed the name "Elizabeth Pierce" in the search field. For the first time. The name was as foreign to me as the name of some Hollywood celebrity who I might have seen in a movie at one time and never heard of again. I had no idea if my mother took her maiden name back after the divorce, and even if she did, I didn't know what it was. Dad never gave me any details about her, and I was never interested in asking. Until this past summer.

Fifteen characters stared back at me, the cursor blinking like it was daring me to hit Enter. My shaking finger hovered over the key. All the chatter and key tapping in the room disappeared, and all I heard was the muffled sound of my heart beating in my ears. My father was nowhere to be seen, but I feared him like he was standing right behind me, watching my every move, knowing every thought in my head.

"Well?" Eden blurted out.

I jumped.

"Did you find her?" Eden scanned the screen. "You haven't done anything yet." She pushed Enter before I could even stop her. "You jump, I jump, right Jack?"

"What?"

"Don't tell me you've never seen *Titanic*?"

"Of course. I just didn't get the reference. I'm a little distracted." I found the courage to look at the monitor. Loads of social media and business profiles with that name popped up. "It looks like we have the same problem."

"Then I'll ask you the same question. Where does she live?"

"No idea."

"Last I heard, my father moved to Texas so I added that to his name." Eden kept her eyes on the screen as she scrolled down the page. "Just start with our state and see what comes up."

I typed in New York before I talked myself out of it. Lots of women with that name lived or once lived in the state, most of them dead, only one sort of local, still alive. I followed the links to the profiles of the living ones and studied their faces.

"Look at all these pictures of my dad." Eden put her face inches from the monitor. "He looks the same as I remember him."

"Where'd you find those?"

"I did an image search, and it took me right to his social media profile. Try it."

Not that it would make a difference because I didn't know what my mother looked like, but I checked the images anyway, scanning the faces for someone who looked like me. There were two possibilities, but I couldn't remember anything about my mom, and I was my father's daughter. I couldn't stop checking over my shoulder and anticipating a smack across the back of my head, making it hard to concentrate. "This isn't working."

"Look, Christa. There he is." She tugged on my arm, practically pulling me off the chair. "With a whole new family." She straightened up and let go of my arm. "He has two new kids, and there's his much younger wife."

"I kind of figured this was a bad idea." I closed the browser window and logged out of the computer. Eden sat next to me, disappointed because she'd found her father; I was disappointed because I didn't even know what to look for. "Are you all right?"

"I'm sick."

I never met her father, but if the photos were any sign, he was a happy man with two happy young kids and a happy wife. That's not what Eden had hoped to find. "Friend him or like him or whatever you're supposed to do."

"I can't do that."

"Why not?"

"He left me, I mean, us, remember?"

"But if he didn't want to be found, don't you think he would've locked down his account? Unless he's totally stupid."

"He's not stupid." Eden scrolled through her father's photo album until she came to the very first picture he ever uploaded. She let out a tiny whimper and buried her face in her hands.

"Let's get out of here."

"No. Look." She tapped the monitor with her finger as tears streamed down her cheeks. There was a picture of a tiny Eden Rhodes perched on her father's lap, and beneath the picture he wrote: "I miss my girl."

"Friend him."

Eden's hands shook. "I can't. Do it for me."

We swapped chairs. I logged into her account as she read off her password.

"Say that it's his daughter and that I miss him, too."

I typed furiously, glancing quickly at the time at the bottom right of the screen. "Done."

Eden jumped out of the chair and raced into the hallway. Even with my long legs, I couldn't keep up with her. She charged down the hall, her arms swinging wildly, stopped, let out a scream, and stomped a foot.

"What's wrong?"

"My own fucking mother fucking lied to me." She flailed her hands and kicked at a locker.

"Stop, before you get in trouble." I dragged her to the bathroom. By then, her face was bright red from hyperventilating. "We can't afford to lose you on the team."

"Really? That's what you're worried about? I'm having a crisis here, in case you haven't noticed."

"It's hard not to notice. But that's just it." I tried to shush her because the bathroom was filled with girls dabbing on lip gloss, sneaking a smoke, or texting. "You don't want them knowing your business."

"I just found out my mother's been lying to me since I was seven, Christa. I don't give a shit about them right now."

Everyone stopped what they were doing and stared at her. Some whispered. Some rolled their eyes.

A toilet flushed and out stepped Janel from a stall. She had the most amazing timing. "What's going on?"

"Mind your own business." I pushed her aside.

She pushed back. "Keep your hands off me. You all right, Eden?"

"No, but I'll be fine." She gave Janel a hug.

"Text me if you need to talk." Janel shot me a nasty look before walking out of the restroom.

Eden nodded and wiped under her eyes with her thumb, smearing her eyeliner a bit.

"I'm not good at this sort of thing," I said, patting her on the shoulder. "Maybe splashing cold water on your face will help."

"I can't go home. I'm too pissed off at my mom." She leaned over the sink, trying to catch her breath. "Can I stay with you tonight?"

Before I even had a chance to think about it, I said, "Sure." My dad still wasn't talking to me, meaning there was no way I could clear it with him first. But he did say

28

she could come over any time, so I could always fall back on his own words as an excuse. Even if I was slowly getting used to this whole rebellious streak growing in me, I was still afraid of his unpredictable anger, but bringing Eden over felt like a subversive way of getting back at him for the birthday humiliation.

"I can't believe she told me he didn't want anything to do with me."

I didn't know what to say. "We're late for class."

"I can't go back looking like this."

"If you don't go to class, Coach Paul won't let you run."

Eden blinked at me a few times. "Is that all you think about?"

"I told you I'm not good at this sort of thing."

"That's right. You did." She threw her backpack over her shoulder and stormed out of the bathroom. "See ya later."

Janel was waiting in the hallway. As soon as she saw Eden, she put her arm around her shoulder and walked her to her next class only a few doors down. They hugged again. I leaned against the wall, watching. Janel caught me glaring at her. She rolled her eyes and walked away. I trailed her. She knew I was there and glanced over her shoulder at me every so often. When she walked faster, so did I. When she stopped and talked with one of our teammates, I stopped and waited. Her next class was on the second floor, and when she reached the stairs, I stood at the bottom and watched her take every. single. step.

"Freak." She flipped me the finger.

I smiled. *Push me aside, will you?*

Ms. Hall glared at me when I walked into anatomy class ten minutes late. "I was about to send a search party out for you."

"I had a little incident."

"I know. I heard. Everyone in the school heard the little incident," she said, making air quotes on little incident. "See me after class."

I nodded, confident I wasn't going to get in trouble for something so small. Nothing was going to happen to me. My reputation for being the best student in the school smoothed things over every time. They trusted me, but then, I never gave them a reason not to trust me.

I told Rachel that Eden had a huge fight with her mother and needed a place to crash for the night. She felt sympathy for the "poor girl," sharing a story of how she fought with her own mother once and ran away. "Don't worry about your father. I'll take care of it," she had said when I called her from school.

Although I got the okay from Rachel, I was a ball of nerves as I pulled in the driveway. Our cross-country practice ran over about an hour. With our first invitational coming up, we were late getting home most days that week. Practice was the only time I was allowed to miss dinner with the family. My father was already home from work and would have had his dinner, thank goodness, so there wouldn't be tense and forced dinner table conversation.

"Take off your shoes and get ready for dinner," Rachel said, as soon as we walked in from the garage. Her voice was high-pitched and sweet. That was her let's-impress-the-guest-and-pretend-everything-is-awesome voice. Normally, she was rather bland and monotone around the house, except when she was slamming pots on the stove and cupboard doors shut.

"We took a shower at school." I untied my shoes and placed them on the rack by the door, along with all the other shoes sitting in a row. I encouraged Eden to do the same. Someone would come along eventually and tuck the strings inside the holes and line the shoes up perfectly — that someone being my father. She didn't say anything when I told her, but I caught a glimpse of an eye roll.

"Rachel, this is my best friend, Eden Rhodes."

Eden did a double-take and mumbled something I couldn't quite make out. "Hey, nice to meet you," she said to Rachel.

"I bet you girls are starving," Rachel said.

"We are," we said together.

"Good, we're eating in the dining room."

I dropped my backpack to the floor. "We?"

"You know your bag doesn't go there. Yes, we. Your father insisted on holding dinner until you came home."

"Oh." I took our bags up the back stairs to my room to avoid eye contact with him until I was ready. I had hoped Eden and I could eat in the kitchen by ourselves without having to put on a show for anyone. The Birthday Bracelet Incident was a week ago, but I expected him to ignore me for at least another month.

"Are you okay?" Eden asked, concerned.

"Let's go before he gets upset."

"Wait." She grabbed hold of my wrist. "Would it be okay if I check to see if my father accepted my friend request on your laptop? I don't have any data left on my phone."

"Shhh, keep your voice down. I'll give you the wi-fi password later. You can check on your phone while I'm doing my homework. We better get going now, though." My father didn't like to be kept waiting, especially when he was hungry. "My stomach is growling."

"Mine, too, but I think it's nerves. What if he doesn't accept my request?"

"Then he's an idiot."

A smile crept across her face as she considered what I said. "You're right. If he doesn't, then he's an idiot, and my mother wasn't lying about him all along."

I heard footsteps coming up the stairs. They were too light for my father's, but I still tensed. I took hold of Eden's hand and started down the hallway. Rachel stood at the top of the steps, eyebrows raised, corner of her mouth lifted to one side.

"Why are you late today?" My father looked to Eden when he asked the question and not at me. Yep, still ignoring me.

"We have a big meet coming up this weekend." Eden twirled spaghetti on her fork and slurped up a mouthful, the noodles leaving sauce on her chin.

My father tapped his chin, laughing.

"I can't eat this stuff without making a mess." She blushed and wiped her mouth. "This is good, Mrs. Pierce."

"Thank you. It's my mother's recipe. And, please, call me Rachel."

"Who are you racing this weekend?" my father said, interrupting the food talk.

I looked up from my plate to find he still wasn't looking to me to answer the questions.

Eden glanced at me then at my father. She didn't know about the birthday dinner and how my father gave me a present and took it right back. "It's an invitational this weekend, so about five schools, I think."

"It's five," I said, keeping my eyes on my plate.

"I see," my father said.

"What do you do for fun, Eden?" Rachel asked. "I mean, other than run cross-country."

"Not much. Between school, work, and running I don't have time for much of anything else."

"Not even a boyfriend?" My father took a sip of wine. "I imagine you have to fight them off with a stick."

"Not really." She lowered her head and looked up at him. "I seem to be every guy's best friend or sister."

"There's nothing wrong with that," Rachel said, her voice a little edgy. She took a gulp of wine.

"I am dating someone, though."

It was nice to have the attention away from me for a change, so I let Eden do all the talking. Instead, I ate my food without having the muscles in my neck clenched tight and enjoyed every single bite. I liked that she could act as a buffer between my father and me whenever she was here. I had hoped my father would disapprove of her so I could irritate him by hanging out with white trash, but I was okay with her taking the pressure off me for a few hours.

I woke up from a nightmare about one o'clock in the morning to find Eden wasn't in her bed. Voices from the kitchen carried up the back stairs straight to my room. One male voice, one female. I tiptoed into the hallway and stood at the top of the steps.

"How old were you when he left?" It was my dad talking to Eden.

"About seven."

"Did your mother tell you why he left?"

"Only that he was a bad parent. Whatever that means."

"I'm so sorry that happened to you. My first wife left me high and dry when Christa was only two years old. She ran off with a much younger man. Guess she wanted a newer model."

Trust my dad to bring the conversation back to him. She was the one worried, waiting for her dad to return

34

her friend request, and there he was milking her for sympathy.

"I imagine Christa talks about it all the time."

The asshole was pumping her for information about me.

"Um, no, she doesn't, actually."

She lied, thank goodness. Good, girl.

"You know you can come to me any time you want to talk. I'm sure you need to talk to someone who understands. I understand exactly what you're going through."

"Thanks. You're a good listener. I better get to bed. This wine is making me sleepy"

He gave her wine?

"Yes, you don't want to fall asleep in class tomorrow."

As soon as I heard the chairs scooting across the kitchen floor, I raced back to bed, facing the wall like I was still asleep. When I heard Eden come in the room, I rolled over and mumbled, "What's going on?"

"I had to pee."

"I thought I heard someone talking."

"I stubbed my toe and started swearing. Sorry for waking you."

I turned and faced the wall, pretending to fall asleep quickly, but I was wide awake. She lied *for* me and then came upstairs and lied *to* me. I didn't like being lied to. Just how much could I trust her? We had only been hanging out for about a month, so I didn't really know her that well, but I thought I was the one in charge of this game.

Four

Eden's father accepted her friend request the next day and explained everything to her in a really long email. She finally gave me the highlights at lunch.

"It sounds like a flimsy excuse, but he said he couldn't handle the responsibility of being a dad when he felt like a kid himself. They were sixteen when they had me. Think of that."

I had thought of it, and it scared the hell out of me, but it had nothing to do with my age. The thought of ever having a kid freaked me out. "That explains why your mom looks so young." My dumb comment went ignored.

"He said he felt like a deadbeat for leaving. My mother refused to let him see me, and he didn't have the money to fight for custody."

I wanted to poke holes in her father's story for some reason. "How did he get to Texas if he didn't have any money?"

"I asked the same thing."

"And?"

"His older brother landed a job on one of the offshore oil rigs and paid for his plane ticket. Dad got a job with the same company, paid off his debts, met someone, and now they have two kids."

My stomach twitched nervously. Eden hadn't seen her father in years, and he had already started a new life without her. My mother left when I was two. Fifteen years was more than enough time to start a new life with a new husband and new kids, maybe even a dog.

"Did you tell your mom?"

"Yep. I thought she'd explode, but she seemed relieved, actually. She said she felt guilty for keeping him away, especially as I got older." She shrugged. "We're talking now so what does it matter?"

"You're so forgiving."

She shrugged again. "When you want something bad enough, you can forgive anyone for just about anything."

"And all that happened in a week."

"I know, right? My head is still spinning. I'm going to Texas for Christmas."

"I thought you were saving your money for a prom dress."

"He's paying my way. Besides, this is more important than a dress."

Explanations, forgiveness, and a paid trip to Texas at Christmas? It was almost too good to believe. I had never seen her so happy, and I was angry at her for it. I thought it was best to keep my expectations in check if I ever met my mom, but boy did Eden make it sound like a lot of fun.

I hated that I was so scared to search for my own mother. While Eden spent the week reconnecting with her father, I spent the week talking myself into looking for her again. Eden told me to keep digging until I found something, but I didn't even know my mother's maiden name, what she looked like, or where she lived. How was I supposed to search for a total stranger? All information about my mother was scrubbed from my life when Dad moved house after the divorce. It was like she'd never existed—no pictures, cards, letters, not even a doodle on a scrap of paper. I had never even seen my birth certificate. Nothing about her was out in the open, if it existed at all anymore. But after listening to Eden's story, jealousy motivated me to want to try anything and everything.

I had always suspected my father was lying to me. Everything he does is a lie. He's a poseur. He lies to Rachel about sleeping with other women. He lies to us about money. He bitched when Rachel asked for three-hundred dollars to chip in on a cruise for her parent's wedding anniversary one day only to drop almost a thousand dollars on a new suit the next. And the bracelet he gave me on my birthday? The one he took back? The one that was so hard to track down and have engraved? I saw it in a flyer for the local jewelry store. It was on sale and cost less than a hundred bucks. If he could lie so easily about small things, it wasn't a stretch to think he'd lied to me about something as big as my mother leaving.

Because my father kept everything in his office neat and tidy, he'd know when something was out of place. He'd know I had touched something I shouldn't. This past week, he had been distracted with work or something and had been coming home later and later each day. Rachel finally got fed up with the late nights and had been hanging out with a friend, walking in the door about a half an hour before he got home so he wouldn't ask questions about where she was and who she was with. It was a stupid game they played with each other, but it was a gift of a chance to go through my father's things, even if it took me days to work up the courage to try it. To be sure I was going to be on my own, I texted both of them to see exactly when they were going to be home. Dad was a question mark but definitely after six; Rachel, within the hour so she could check on the dinner in the slow cooker.

From the age of three or so, when I had been a grabby little kid, I was told to stay out of his office. To be sure I would listen, he would lock the door. I used to stand on my tip-toes, wishing I could reach the door handle to open it. Something about him telling me to stay out made his office more attractive to me. By the time I could reach the handle, I knew better than to open it.

The hinges snapped as I pushed the door open an inch. The sound amplified in the quiet house. Certain my father heard me from wherever he was, I stepped backwards, pulling the door closed, my sweaty palms slipping off the knob. I took a couple of deep breaths.

This was nuts. I couldn't do it. He'd know. He always knows.

I thought of Eden. She had found her father and reconnected with him. No, it wasn't the same situation, but it was close. I couldn't imagine my mother didn't want to see me or have anything to do with me. It wasn't possible. It was a lie, just another of Dad's lies. Maybe I believed it when I was younger but not now, not after living with my his lies every day. And yet, I couldn't find courage in that realization. What would Eden do if she were in my situation, if she were standing where I was standing? She would do it. She would do it and not care what the consequences were. She was brave and confident, and I was nothing more than a chicken shit.

The problem with snooping was remembering to put everything back exactly how I found it. If I took a picture of how it looked before I touched it, then I could put it back exactly the way it was and erase the pictures from my phone.

I had forty-five minutes.

If my father were hiding evidence of my mother's existence from me, where would he hide it? Because he was an anal-retentive sort of man, papers would be with papers, photos would be with photos, and whatever. And where were all the papers? In his desk or filing cabinet. I grabbed a towel from the kitchen to erase my fingerprints and started looking around. To my surprise, his desk was unlocked.

I opened one drawer and snapped a picture before rummaging around. His desk was mostly filled with important papers of boring stuff, business junk, and one drawer full of office supplies and a ring full of keys, but nothing to do with my mother.

A tall, beat up, gray filing cabinet sat next to his laser printer. I yanked on the top drawer and nearly pulled my shoulder out of joint. It was locked. Locked things always meant secrets to me. So that's why there was a bunch of keys in his desk.

I tried the first one on the keyring that didn't look like a house key and jammed it in the keyhole good and tight. Of course, I did. Why wouldn't I do something so stupid? My heart raced at the thought of Dad coming home and finding the keyring dangling from the lock of his filing cabinet. There were only two people who would be snooping through his stuff, and it wouldn't take long to figure out it wasn't Rachel.

"Shit, shit, shit!" I steadied my breath. "Calm down, dumbass." I lifted and twisted and pulled at the key until it finally gave. Next time, I wouldn't be so careless. I tried one key after another on that stupid filing cabinet, worried that it was eating into my snooping time. Not only was I running out of time, but I was running out of keys. Two keys left. I slipped the second to the last in and it turned. Finally. I giggled, quickly slapping my hand over my mouth. The drawers were filled with hanging folders labeled with things like *Mortgage* and *Retirement*. More boring shit. I kept going.

I made it to the bottom drawer, deflated. This was the last obvious hiding place, unless he kept stuff hidden in his bedroom closet. And when would I have time to snoop there?

Way at the back of the bottom drawer I found a worn manila envelope. Inside was every one of my school pictures from kindergarten up until my senior year. There was also another picture among them. My hands shook. It was a picture of my mother and my father and me, not one of us smiling or even faking it. I must have been about a year old. But there she was. Petite, brown hair, blue eyes, and olive skin. I didn't look anything like her. I smiled, tears blurring my vision. "She's beautiful."

On the back of the photo there was a Post-it with an address written on it. I snapped a picture of the photo of my mom, the address, and put everything back into place, put the keys back in the desk drawer, and wiped my fingerprints off of whatever I'd touched.

What was I supposed to do? Whose address was this? I had twenty minutes left before Rachel came home.

I ran to my room, fired up my laptop, and started typing the address in the search field but stopped myself. Dad told me he had tracking software on my computer and could see what I was doing online, in case I ever planned to hook-up with a boy. I called Eden. She'd know what to do.

"Hey, are you busy?"

"Kind of. I'm messaging with my father. You sound funny. What's wrong?"

"I found an address in my...when I was searching... Could you check it out for me? It doesn't have a city, just a street."

"Can't you do it yourself?"

"Not here. We're supposed to keep this at school. Remember?"

"Ooooh, that. I'm not even going to ask. What is it?"

I read off the address in a whisper and heard her fingers typing furiously.

"Google Earth says there's a street of that name in Ruffsdale." She paused. "Is that your mother's address? How'd you find it? Never mind. I said I wasn't going to ask."

"I don't have time to explain, anyway. Ruffsdale is only an hour away, right?"

"More like two hours. What are you going to do?"

"What do you think I'm going to do?"

"That's a bad idea."

"Why? You did it."

"Yeah, through email. I didn't show up at his house." She let out an exasperated sigh. "Don't do anything to get yourself in trouble."

The garage door opening rumbled the floor of my bedroom. "Gotta go."

I scribbled the address in my AP history notebook, buried among class notes so he wouldn't find it. I took a long look at the picture of my mother before erasing all the pictures from my phone. My body surged with nervous energy, making me feel alive, powerful, and big. Big like a giant. I could see myself crushing

44

everything under my giant feet, crushing skulls, like my dad's. My whole life I had been afraid of that man, and for the first time ever, I felt like I could hit him with my giant hands if he were only standing in front of me.

Just as Eden's father had an explanation for what had happened, I was sure my mother had a different story to tell, far different from what my father had fed me since I was a little girl. I wanted to hear her side of things.

Would the outcome be as exciting as Eden's was, or was I setting myself up for an embarrassing disappointment?

Five

I had never skipped a single day of school in my life. Unless I had a fever of 101° or higher, my father made me go to class. Most seniors skipped a day or two without getting grilled by the teachers. It was sort of a rite of passage, but getting on a bus to look for the woman who'd abandoned me was more than cutting class to get my nails done at the mall.

I could have taken my car, but that felt too risky to me. If, for some reason, Dad happened to be out for lunch or at a meeting somewhere off campus and spotted my car, he'd rip me to shreds later. Taking the bus felt safer. This way he'd never know what I had done.

I parked at the far edge of the student parking lot at school, which was down the hill and out of sight from the main entrance to the building, giving any student an easy way to escape. Since most of the students who drove to school showed up mere minutes before homeroom bell, I got there about ten minutes earlier, just as the buses started rolling in.

I changed into sweats and a hoodie in the car, climbed out the passenger side door, slid down the hill until I was out of view of the school, and ran the mile to the bus station downtown. With my build, I was just another guy out for an early morning run.

Dad wouldn't be caught dead on this side of town, yet I couldn't stop looking over my shoulder. When a red Mercedes like my father's drove by, I ducked into an alley, my heart pounding in my chest as I struggled to catch a breath. I laughed. The adrenaline coursing through my body fueled me in strange new ways.

Soaked in sweat and out of breath, I finally made it to the bus station and bought a round-trip ticket to Ruffsdale before I talked myself out of it. Two hours one way and two hours back didn't leave me much time to find and, hopefully, talk with my mother. So many times I had fantasized about having a moment like this, but now that I was so close to getting it, I didn't know what I could possibly say to her or how I was going to react when I saw her, if I saw her, or if I could even find her. Before I left the house, I made a promise to myself to keep my expectations in check. Before I left the house, I had a lot more courage than I did while waiting to board the bus.

What was I doing? If she'd wanted to see me, she would have tried. Wouldn't she? What would keep a mother away from her kid?

A boarding announcement crackled over the intercom. There was no turning back. Muscles in my body twitched as I stood in line to get on the bus. It was the same feeling I got when I was about to start a race so I was used to the sensation, but this wasn't a race. My legs didn't want to move, despite my muscles firing on all cylinders. A voice behind me mumbling, *Hurry up!* kicked me into gear. I was doing this. I scanned the faces of everyone nearby one more time before boarding. Strangers, all of them. My face mostly hidden under the hood of my sweatshirt, no one would remember seeing me.

For the next two hours, I stared out the window, watching cars and neighborhoods whiz by to distract myself from worry. It didn't work. What would I say to her? What will we talk about? Will she be happy to see me or will she reject me like she did before?

My father would call the neighborhood my mother lived in bohemian. He would say it with a sneer on his face and derision in his voice. The streets were filled with art galleries, head shops, coffee shops, and used bookstores. This place had more of a college-town vibe to it than my own did. I stopped at one of the coffee shops and asked for directions to the address I found on the back of the family photo. It would have been easier to use the GPS on my phone, but since Dad tracked my activities, I didn't dare.

"It's about two miles from here." The barista, a softly-round woman with bright red curly hair, gave me detailed directions, even writing them down on a napkin for me. "I live a couple of streets over. Do you want me to call a taxi for you?"

"No, I can walk, thanks." If this woman lived a couple of streets over, maybe she knew my mother. I ordered a cup of coffee and a chocolate croissant. "Do you know the woman who lives there?"

She nodded, passing the cup and pastry off to me. "She's a good friend."

What a lucky coincidence for me but not really surprising. Ruffsdale was a small town, after all. But since she knew the woman who lived there, I had to ask.

"Does her family live with her?" *Please say no.*

"No." She smiled again. It was a weird kind of smile, like she had some secret joke that I wasn't in on and was laughing at me on the inside. "Her family doesn't live with her."

Unsure of what to say, I nodded and smiled.

"Cream and sugar are over there in the corner."

"Thanks." I started to walk away.

"Do you know her, the woman who lives there?" the barista said, with a hint of curious concern in her voice.

If I said no, I'd be mistaken for a creeper. If I said yes, she might ask even more questions and make me trip up in my own lies. But what choice did I have? "Yes, but I haven't seen her in a long time."

She glanced at the clock on the wall behind her. "I know she teaches a class in a few hours so you might want to hurry on over. You sure you don't want me to call for a ride?"

"No, I'm good."

I shoved the croissant in my mouth as I spilled six packs of sugar and a good helping of cream in my cup. I pretended to take a gulp of the coffee on the way out the door. The pastry would sit on my stomach just fine—it wasn't like I had never eaten right before a run—but the coffee was debatable. As soon as I was out of sight of the coffee shop, I dropped the cup in the first trash can I saw and broke into a steady eight-minute-mile pace.

My mother a teacher? Knowing she was home twisted me up inside. It was a good thing I didn't have that coffee. Excited, nervous, scared out of my freaking mind, happy, sad—I was all over the emotional map. My legs seemed detached from the rest of me. Watching them move and hearing my feet hit the pavement was the only way I knew I was really moving, moving closer to her.

The face of the neighborhood changed as I got closer to her house. I half expected to see the houses getting bigger and prettier, but it was the opposite. The yards were small and dumpy, the houses old and rundown. My mother was poor. When I got within a few blocks of her street, I stopped running to catch my breath before meeting her. I was wrong about the croissant. My stomach churned from nerves and two miles of shallow breathing. Now I understood how Eden felt while she waited for her father to accept her friend request. Would my mother accept me?

I stood on the sidewalk outside my mother's house and waited for the courage to walk up the steps and knock on her door. The yard was clean and full of miniature sunflowers hanging onto their last breath of summer. To my surprise, the front door swung open, and a woman walked out and stood at the edge of the porch. There she was.

"You better come inside before someone sees you."

I still had the hood up over my head—I could have been anyone, but she knew who I was. All those years of fantasizing about this very moment couldn't prepare me for it. What was I supposed to say to her? I started to walk away. I wasn't at all ready for this. If I had actually thought this through, I would have realized I never would be prepared to meet her.

"Don't go. Please. I just made some tea."

My legs moved toward the door without any help from my brain. Before I knew it, I was on the porch, standing face-to-face with the woman I didn't remember being my mother. I peeled the hood off my head.

She gasped and covered her mouth. "Christa. When Sydney phoned that a young girl was asking about me at the coffee shop, I didn't want to get my hopes up. I can't believe this." Her whole body shook, and I just stood there watching her.

"Why did you leave me?" The words came out with such force that she got control of herself quickly.

"I figured he'd tell you some bullshit story." She wiped her face dry and looked me up and down, smiling through the tears. "We have a lot to talk about."

"Can you explain fifteen years in an hour and a half?"

"No, but I can try. Can I at least hug you?"

She collapsed in my arms and sobbed before I could even answer yes or no. I didn't know what to feel. Fifteen years of mixed messages and lies from my father left me confused. Slowly, I inched my arms around her and inhaled. I missed this woman, and in that moment, I realized how much.

"We better get inside." She sniffled. Her eyes and nose were red, her face splotched. "Hungry?"

"Not sure I can eat right now."

"That's all right. Come in." I followed her to a cramped kitchen and sat at her small table. "I had hoped and prayed for this very thing to happen for years, but now that you're here, I don't know what to say or where to start. How did you find me? I'm sure your father didn't give you my address."

"I snooped through his things."

"Good for you. How do you like your tea?"

"Any way is fine." I was a ball of nerves. What I didn't need was more caffeine, but I didn't want to reject the first offer of kindness from her. "You said you figured Dad would tell me some bullshit story. What do you mean?"

She placed a cup in front of me as well as a plate of cookies. "I can see you want to skip the get-to-know-you segment of the program and get right to the good stuff."

"I need to know the truth."

She folded her hands in front of her and gazed into my eyes. She looked a little different in person than the woman in the picture—different hairstyle, a few grays, more wrinkles especially around the eyes.

"Tell me your side of the story."

"The condensed version: your father cheated, his verbal abuse escalated, and I didn't want to raise you in that environment. When I tried to leave with you, he had me declared an unfit mother. He trumped up kidnapping charges, told the court I was a drug addict, got a restraining order against me, and I lost you for good. I almost went to jail."

My father was an intense man, abusive to me, sure, but this sounded too outrageous to believe. Kidnapping charges? Restraining order? "Why would he do that?"

"Because Michael Pierce doesn't like to lose, least of all to a woman."

"But it was only a divorce."

"A divorce that I, a poor housewife, initiated. Think of the hit to his public image, especially with the dirt I had on him."

"Like what?"

"The cheating mostly. Not so much how many women but who they were. Look, I don't want you to get involved. Just know that no matter what I did right it wasn't enough." She started crying again. "I missed out on everything, and it's all my fault."

"It doesn't sound like your fault to me. I know what he's like. But why didn't you hire a lawyer?"

"Where would I get the money to fight him and his powerful connections? I only had enough money to file for divorce. I was penniless and uneducated when I left. If it weren't for my sister, I would've been homeless."

I jumped up out of the chair and paced the kitchen. "He said you didn't want to have anything to do with me. He said you left because of some guy who didn't want to be burdened with a kid so you left me behind."

She shook her head. "I didn't leave you. There was no guy. He destroyed me, and I didn't have the money to fight for you. I almost got thrown in jail."

That was starting to sound more like an excuse than an explanation. "Would he have let that happen?"

"I thought you knew your father."

My head spinning, I hugged myself. I was in my mother's house, in my mother's kitchen. The woman I had phantom memories of sat at the table, telling me what I suspected all along.

"You're here now, though, and I want to get to know you, make up for lost time."

"But what about two years ago or five? Why didn't you try then?"

"I did. I used to sneak to your cross-country meets when you first started high school, but every time I was found out. Within a few days I had some goon threaten me to stay away or else. Even your being here now puts my life in danger."

"Mine, too. If he finds out I'm here, he'll…"

She darted up and took me by the shoulders. "He's hitting you?"

I nodded, too ashamed to look her in the eye.

54

"I'm so sorry. You have to believe me that I was powerless to stop him. If I could, I would have. Let me show you something. Have a seat."

My mother fetched something from a small bookshelf in her tiny living room. She took a seat at the table and placed a book in front of her like it contained sacred text. She rested her hand on top of it and stared at me like she was thinking of what to say next.

I couldn't handle the quiet of her house any longer. "What is it?"

She pushed the book toward me. "You'll have even more questions, and I'll answer them as best I can."

The cardboard cover squeaked against the spiral binding as I opened it. On the first page was a picture of me when I started kindergarten. On the back of that page were photocopies of those meaningless awards you get for just showing up. Next was my first grade picture along with a copy of my report card. Then second grade, third grade, all the way through to my junior year. My mother beamed with pride. "How did you get these?"

"From an unlikely source. Rachel."

That explained what I found in the filing cabinet. "How long has this been going on?"

"About three years ago, I got a package in the mail with all these pictures and report cards and drawings. It was from some law firm. I didn't question it, but the packages kept coming in the mail. She even made copies of videos of you. I wore them out watching them." She reached for my hand. "I want you to know I never gave up on trying to get to you. Every time I tried, he retaliated. My house was broken into and ransacked three times. I was mugged once. Threatened with rape. Each time the message was loud and clear: stay away!"

"Why didn't you just go to the police?"

Sadness washed over her face. She slumped in the chair and suddenly looked so small and broken, defeated. "I'm afraid of him. Rachel's afraid of him. You're afraid. Look at you. You haven't relaxed since you came in my house. I bet you looked over your shoulder the entire way here."

I couldn't deny it.

"I have so much to tell you, so much time to make up for, but it's never going to happen as long as you're living with him."

"I'll go to college in California or something. I'll work three jobs if I have to."

"You should get as far away from him as you can, and wherever you go, I'll go. We can start over. Together we can make it." Her eyes came alive as she talked about all these wild and crazy plans for the future. "Now that I have you back in my life, how are we going to make this work?"

"I'll just sit down and talk with him." Even I didn't believe it was possible, but it sounded good coming out of my mouth. "I'm seventeen. I should be able to have my own mother in my life if I want. He can't keep us apart forever."

My mother wasn't convinced, either. She tilted her head to the side and covered her mouth with her hand. "Don't get yourself in trouble."

"I don't have to do much for that to happen."

"Do you have an email address?" She grabbed a notepad off the counter and waited for me to respond.

"I'll have to check from school. Dad spies on my internet activities." I checked the time on the clock on the microwave. "I have to go if I want to catch the bus."

"I don't want you to leave, but I'm so happy you came."

"What should I call you?"

"What do you want to call me?"

I shrugged. "I don't know."

"You can call me whatever you want. How's that?"

"It feels weird to call you Elizabeth." I threw my arms around her. "Bye, Mom." Even that felt weird. I ran out of the house before I started crying. I had thirty minutes to get to the bus station and two hours to seethe in rage as I thought about how my father kept my mother from me.

The stories he told me ran through my head. She left because of me. She picked the new guy over me because he didn't want to be saddled with someone else's kid. She never loved me as much as he did. She didn't have the maternal instinct, he said. Lies. All of it. I was only in her house for a short while and felt more love in that time than I ever had living with my father.

The two-hour bus ride back home gave me a lot of time to think. Dad had the final word on everything. He made decisions for me, influenced how I thought, what I wore, how I treated other people, how I saw myself. I was so afraid of him that I didn't know how to stand up for myself to even stop his control. Lately, though, that fear had been turning into something else. Every so often, a thought like hitting him over the head with a shovel or running him over with my car would pop into my head, and I would get this rush of excitement or adrenaline—I didn't know which. But then, instead of getting sick at the thought, I'd catch myself smiling or giggling. Once, in the middle of Calculus, I snorted out loud when I imagined watching him choke to death on a piece of chicken.

When the bus rolled through a tunnel, I saw my reflection in the window. I was smiling again.

Six

The house was dark. Most of the window blinds were closed, the lights off. The spicy smell of chili filled the air as I lifted the lid of the slow cooker. The house had an unnerving stillness to it that normally would have had me worried. But Rachel was nowhere in sight, and neither was my dad. I took a long inhale and blew it out slowly, forcing my shoulders down from my ears, grateful for some alone-time to decompress after a weird day.

Sometimes I had a hard time naming feelings, and this was one of those times. My mind whirled with memories of the smell of my mother's house, her clothes, hair, the sound of her voice, and the strength of her hugs. These thoughts stirred something in me that made me itch from the inside out.

After being on that awful bus with all those stinky people, I was glad to come home to an empty house. It would give me time to process what I was feeling, thinking, planning. I kicked one shoe off, trying to make a basket in the garbage can. It bounced off the side and landed on the floor with a smack. I flung the other one, trying to score a point, but ended up hitting the wall instead making an even louder smack.

"Enough with the games, Christa." My father's voice shot out of nowhere.

I felt a squirt in my pants before my body clenched up completely. "Dad?"

"Who did you think it was?" The leather of his favorite chair squeaked as he stood up. He walked in the kitchen calmly, deliberately, and leaned against the doorway with his hands in his pockets.

"What are you doing here?" I stammered, finding it hard to breathe and talk at the same time.

"Yes, what am I doing here?" His voice oozed with anger, but he wasn't yelling. The message was unmistakable, though.

Of course, I got caught. It didn't matter what I did, somebody was always watching me, just like he told me time and time again. But how did he find out? I'd been careful. Told no one.

"Where's Rachel?"

Whenever the punishment was severe, my father chased her out of the house so she wouldn't witness it, hear it, or try to stop it. Not that she ever did.

He walked up to me slowly and slapped me across the face, knocking me into the kitchen table. I braced myself for the next blow. I knew better than to reach up and touch my cheek. It was a sign of weakness. I'd learned that long ago.

"I'll ask the questions." He methodically pulled out a chair and sat down. "It's bad enough that you're the offspring of that stupid bitch. That can't be helped. I kept my mouth shut when you brought that tramp Eden home with you, but don't think you can get away with lying to me."

I swallowed hard, the muscles in my throat so tight I could have choked on my own saliva. My cheek burned from the slap. Pain stabbed my leg where my thigh had hit the edge of the table. My body stiffened, making it hard to breathe He wasn't done. He wasn't getting out of the room and walking away. I stayed leaning over the table and waited.

"I hate it when people betray me, Christa. How many times do I have to tell you that someone knows everything you do? Do you think I make these things up? Life is hard. This world isn't safe. Someone is out there waiting for you to slip up, to make one simple mistake. You can't let your guard down. The minute you do someone will be there. And guess what? You slipped up."

Let's get this over with, was all I could think.

He stood up unhurriedly, unbuckling his belt and folding it in half neatly. He leaned over and whispered in my ear, his hot breath tickling my neck. "Tonight, when you're alone in your room, you can ask yourself this question: Was skipping school to visit my mother and deceiving my father worth it?"

I braced myself against the table.

I didn't cry.

It took ten minutes to peel my underwear off. I fought to catch a breath after every try until I finally got brave enough to do it in one shot. There was no way in hell that I'd give him the satisfaction of knowing he'd hurt me and how bad. Over the years, I'd learned to breathe through the pain of his slap, his belt buckle, his fist, his body slam into the wall. And so I breathed.

But I didn't cry.

I thought I'd try something new this time around. Instead of putting ice packs on my backside, I'd sit in a tub of cold water. As the water ran, I stood with my back toward the mirror to see the damage: two-inch-wide red and purple welts across my ass and the back of my thighs. As cuts and bruises and welts went, this beating was by far the worst and left the most damage. I counted eight stripes. I tuned out and stopped counting after the second hit. It had been such a long time since he'd beat me with his belt that I'd forgotten the pain of the last one. I thought he'd stop when I got older.

I eased into the water, holding my breath as the shock of cold against my hot and swollen skin hit me. I couldn't sit down on the hard porcelain, so I kneeled in the tub, hanging my butt in the water with my teeth chattering. Was it worth it, Daddy? Yes. And I would do it again in a nano-second knowing how much you'd hated it.

Rachel came home not long after the incident. The clanging and banging of dishes and silverware in the kitchen traveled upstairs. Between water drips, I listened to her trying to get my father to talk, but by the sound of it, he wasn't having it. This went on for a good twenty minutes, until her high-pitched nervous rambling finally stopped and his deep mumbles started. It was a short speech, and I couldn't make out any of it, but before long Rachel marched upstairs and knocked on the door. "Dinner will be ready in twenty minutes."

"Thanks." My voice trembled.

"We're eating in the kitchen." She paused. "Your father's suggestion."

Except for breakfast and lunch, we always ate in the dining room. The dining room chairs were padded. The chairs in the kitchen were not. And I was expected to sit at the table with the rest of the family, to have a normal conversation, eat everything on my plate, act like nothing was wrong, that the chairs weren't making the pain worse, and that I didn't hate my father for what he did.

I toweled off softly and slipped into a pair of baggy sweatpants, no underwear. I made my way downstairs, my father watching my every move like the sadist he was. He smiled. I returned the smile as I eased myself onto the chair next to his.

I didn't cry, you monster.

Rachel ladled chili into each bowl with a shaky hand and passed it off to us. "There's sour cream, chives, and fresh cheddar cheese for toppings. I know how much you love cheese, Christa."

"It looks good." My voice might have trembled earlier, but I made sure to punch the words out with as much force as I could muster this time. Life with Dad taught me to suck it up and fake it.

"There was a time when all you wanted was chili." She couldn't even look me in the eye. "Do you want butter or margarine for the cornbread?" She skittered off and rummaged around in the refrigerator. "I think this margarine is outdated." She was trying too hard, and I could see by my father's expression that it was getting on his nerves. "Who wants to be brave and try it?"

"Butter's fine, Rach." Dad blinked slowly, growling a little.

"All right, butter it is. Would anyone like some wine?"

Wine with chili? Gross. But with one glass of wine, I could catch a light buzz. If I were lucky, he wouldn't notice, and I could drink two glasses. And maybe after everyone had gone to bed I could sneak into the kitchen and drink the rest. I wanted to be numb. I looked to my father for a nod of approval before saying yes.

"Aren't you going to ask how my day was, Princess?" He shoved a piece of cornbread in his mouth.

I looked him dead in the eye. "How was your day, Daddy?" I took a swig of wine. It burned going down, but it didn't take long before the alcohol crept through my veins and calmed me.

"I've been nominated for an Excellence in Public Service award. Isn't that exciting?"

"That is exciting." Rachel gushed over the announcement, clapping her hands and giggling like a little kid who had been given the best toy ever. I took another swig of wine.

My father ate slowly. On purpose. He saw me squirming, struggling to get comfortable in my chair. I wasn't allowed to ask to be excused after a punishment, so his idea of fun was to drag the meal out as long as possible. I took larger bites of the chili, hoping to end the agony quicker. Maybe if he saw me eating faster, he would too.

Between bites, I sucked down more wine. My head grew heavy, and I struggled to keep my eyes focused as I put the last spoonful to my lips. There. Finished. Dad ladled another helping of chili into my bowl. I focused on the dark red mess with its little beads of grease floating on top, trying not to give him the satisfaction of a reaction. I finished the second helping off in five large bites. By then, I was not only drunk, I was about to burst.

With his eyes narrowed and a crooked smile, he placed a piece of cornbread in the bowl and folded his hands under his chin. He leaned forward and watched as I ate the bread. Feeling emboldened by the wine, I met his gaze. My eyes felt droopy, but I saw him clearly.

He frowned and pushed himself away from the table. "You may be excused."

I could barely breathe I was so full, and I thought I was going to barf right there on the table.

Rachel nudged me with her foot. "Get upstairs. Now."

The room spun as I stood. Rachel took my arm and dragged me to the powder room just in time for me to spray everything in the toilet.

"Better?" She still couldn't look me in the eyes. I wanted to grab her and ask why she was staying with him when he was such an abusive asshole, but I still felt sick. She turned the water on and guided my head toward the sink. "Splash some cold water on your face and take a sip to rinse your mouth out."

I swooshed the water around in my mouth and spit it in the toilet. It felt good to throw up. I didn't feel full anymore, but I still had a buzz from the alcohol.

"Get upstairs and lock the door."

How did Dad find out?

I was a senior, so I doubt anyone from school called to ask him where I was. But then I never missed a day until today, and maybe my absence worried one of the teachers. I doubted it. No one we knew saw me. I wasn't followed. I kept checking over my shoulder and didn't recognize anyone. No one trailed me, I was sure of it. No one knew I was going to find my mother.

Except Eden.

Seven

By morning, the belt marks on my backside had turned to dark purple and red bruises. I'd learned to cover the evidence of my beatings with clothes depending on where I got hit. Bruises on my arm where he twisted my wrist? Wear a long-sleeved shirt. Scratches on my neck where his fingernails dug into my skin as I jerked out of his clutches? Turtleneck.

I pulled a long, flowy skirt out of the closet. The elastic of my underwear cut into my puffy skin, but the fabric of the skirt was soft and wouldn't bunch up or dig in when I sat down. Sitting in class all day was going to be real fun. And then I had to run after school. My hamstrings and glutes were already stiff from the hits. I was glad it was cold outside so I could wear sweatpants for the run, but the bouncing around and fabric rubbing against my legs was going to hurt. I popped a couple of aspirin, stuffing the bottle in my purse for later, and chased them down with plain toast and tea. My throat was still raw from throwing up last night's dinner, so it didn't go down easy. *Still worth it, Daddy*.

Considering what I had done, I was surprised I only got the belt. I wasn't grounded. I could still drive my car.

He didn't tell me to stop seeing Eden. That was the way it always was, though. Being grounded, not hanging out with schoolmates, having privileges taken away was obvious to the outside world. People would notice those things, and if they noticed, they'd ask questions. Questions were dangerous. Questions meant someone was curious and suspicious. It meant they could see through the façade, and we couldn't have that.

I climbed into the car, breathing in and out deeply as I adjusted to the pain of my ass in the seat. It hadn't been long enough for the pain pills to work, but by the time I got to school, I felt a little better.

As I headed to my locker, Eden came bouncing down the hallway toward me. My face burned with anger at the sight of her. She was the only one who knew I was going to visit my mother. She was the only one who would have told on me. It had to have been her. But why would she do that? Why would she tell my father anything?

"Did you find her?" Eden asked, excited.

"Yes." I didn't elaborate or look into her face.

"Well? How did it go?"

"Fine." The warning bell rang, saving me from answering more of her questions.

Eden jumped up and down, squealing like she had won a million-dollar prize. "This is so exciting. You have to tell me everything after school. You look nice today, by the way. I can't remember the last time I saw you in something other than khakis or sweats. What's his name?"

68

"I need to run to the computer lab before homeroom." I said, ignoring her question.

"You won't have time. Why don't we meet there for lunch?"

"Because all the little freshmen are there during our lunch period."

"You won't be able to do it any other time."

"Yeah, you're right."

"Are you okay? You seem mad about something."

"Why would I be mad?" I stared so hard into her eyes, I could have bored a hole through her skull with the intensity.

Eden threw her hands up and shrugged. "I don't know. That's why I'm asking."

The second bell rang just in time. "I'll see you later."

My mother had sent me three emails. I bounced my legs nervously, causing the table to shake. The guy on the computer across from me popped his head around the monitor and shot me a dirty look. My mind raced, wanting to read all three at the same time. As I was about to open the first email, Eden plopped down beside me in a huff.

I didn't take my eyes off the screen. "What's wrong?"

"Nothing."

"You were fine this morning. What happened?"

"You can be mad about stuff, so why can't I?"

She was out of breath and sweaty, her hands shaky. Her cheeks and nose were red, like she'd been crying. As she fanned her face with her hands, I caught a glimpse of something shiny on her left wrist. I had to blink a couple of times to be sure I wasn't imagining things. Partially covered by her shirtsleeve, I was still able to recognize the embossed roses on the edges of the plate. I couldn't breathe. The excitement I felt over the emails from my mother disappeared in an instant.

Was she wearing *my* bracelet?

Sure, it was a common enough bracelet. I'd found it in the Sunday flyer for the local jewelry store, but I knew she couldn't afford it. Maybe Kyle bought it for her.

I swallowed the lump in my throat. "How are things with you and Kyle?"

She didn't answer right away. "Good."

That wasn't a convincing answer. "Is he still taking you to prom?"

"Prom is months away, but if we're still together, sure." She pulled the sleeve down over her wrist, covering the bracelet. "I have to write up this stupid book report before eighth period." She stuffed her earbuds in and ignored me.

I stared at my mother's name on the screen, my brain caught in a hitch. I didn't know what to do: question Eden about the bracelet, demanding the truth, or forget about it and read the emails from my mother. The bracelet had to be a coincidence. Anyone could have that bracelet. I repeated the word coincidence in my head until I regained focus.

I opened the first email: *Christa, you were so brave to come and see me. I hope your visit doesn't come back to bite either of us in the rear-end. So far, so good here. No goons, no threatening phone calls, no one...*

It was pointless to continue. My brain couldn't let go of the bracelet around Eden's wrist.

The other girls, especially Janel, wondered why I was hiding in the bathroom stall instead of getting dressed near my locker. I didn't want anyone to see the bruises and red marks on my backside, but I couldn't tell them that. That was a Pierce family secret, so I told them I was on my period and had to use the bathroom. This excuse came in handy later when the girls showered and I didn't.

Janel, Miko, and Leesa were nosy, asking Eden all sorts of intrusive questions about Kyle and what their plans were after graduation. While all the other girls were showering and talking non-stop, I snooped through Eden's bag. She didn't have the bracelet on during the run, so she must have stashed it somewhere in her things.

Eden had left her bag wide open on the bench near her locker. She was always careless like that. She wouldn't notice something missing from her bag until it was too late. Since the locker was out of sight from the showers, I dug in furiously. The bracelet wasn't in her jeans pocket, or the pocket of her bag, or in her shoe or sock. I searched her purse. In the little side pocket where she kept lip balm and condoms, I found it.

My hand shook as I pulled it out of its hiding place. The conversation in the shower room was wrapping up, so I had to move quickly.

I flipped it over and saw the three words that would only mean something to me and my father: "For My Princess." It slipped out of my hand and fell to the floor. My ears started ringing, and my head felt like it was about to explode.

I felt sicker than the night I threw up all the food Dad forced me to eat. Sicker than when I found out he lied to me about my mother. Sicker than the first time I found out he brought his mistresses into the house.

Showers were turning off. Leesa's loud giggles grew louder, followed by wet feet squeaking in flip-flops across the cement floor. I fumbled for the bracelet lying at my feet, put it back where I found it, stuffed Eden's clothes back in her bag, and raced to my car.

I drove home in a blur. It was a weird sensation to lose time, not remembering how I got from school to home. Rachel must have noticed something was off and asked if I was feeling all right.

"I have cramps. I'll be in my room."

"I'll bring you something to eat later." She was always super nice to me after a belt incident. I never wanted her pity, but it was hard to resent her, knowing what she did for my mother. She was the bridge between my mother and me, a bridge my father didn't know about. She kept that secret from him all these years, and it was a dangerous secret to keep from the likes of Michael Pierce.

Halfway up the stairs, I turned and raced back to the kitchen. "Why don't you leave him?" I was surprised at the force behind my words, but everything looked different now than it did a week ago, and I had nothing to lose.

The question must have thrown her sideways. She kind of laughed, kind of considered it, and kind of tried to dismiss it at the same time. "It's not that easy." She sounded so defeated, sort of how my mother sounded when she talked about my father.

"Sure it is. You're an adult. You have options."

Her eyes narrowed. "Do I?"

"Uh, yeah."

She slammed the oven door shut. "Do you know how sick I am of hearing how easy it is to leave? You can't always just walk away. He bled me dry, Christa. That's what he does. He takes everything until one day you wake up and find you have nothing. What little money I had when I came into this marriage is now gone. He won't even let me get a job. He won't *let* me! Think of that. When you don't have money, you don't have power. When you don't have power, he has control. Ask your mother. She'll tell you."

As much as I wanted to talk about my mother with her and thank her for what she did, I decided not to bring it up. I wanted to keep something for myself, something that wasn't tainted by anyone else in this house. I wanted her to be mine and mine alone.

"But don't worry about me. I've got something in the works. Everyone thinks I'm dumb and blind to what he's doing, but I'm not. I'm scared, Christa. You're not the only one being abused around here. He already told me what would happen if I left him. Do you understand?"

I nodded slowly.

"Maybe you should take your own advice and get out when you can."

"He won't even let me choose which college I want to go to. Where does that leave me? Stuck here, like you."

"After you graduate, leave. Don't worry about college for a year. Just go away, and don't ever look back."

"You make it sound so simple." After the words left my mouth, I wanted to take them back, embarrassed by the irony.

"Now you understand."

We heard the garage door open at the same time and snapped back to the reality of our lives. Rachel finished cooking dinner, pretending everything was right with the world. I sprinted upstairs to my room and seethed with anger.

Eight

The rest of the week, I thought of nothing else but that bracelet. The sight of it on Eden's wrist. Her covering it up like it was no big deal. Finding it in her bag. Over and over in my brain. The obsession fueled me during our meet that weekend, and our school ended up winning thanks to me.

After a big race, I usually crashed, but not this time. I couldn't keep still. Dad and Rachel were busy working on his acceptance speech for the awards banquet in a few weeks, so I was mostly on my own. The mood in the house was light. I always took advantage of that and did things I wouldn't normally do, like watching cartoons on Saturday morning, or staying up late to catch an old movie, or breathing. But nothing interested me. Something nagged me.

It wasn't a coincidence, that bracelet. It couldn't have been. My father must have given it to her. I may not have been close friends with Eden very long, but nobody called her Princess. Not her mother, not Kyle, and definitely not her father. I overheard her telling Janel that his nickname for her had always been Nugget because she was short. Besides, if the bracelet was a present from anyone close to her, especially her father, she would have told me, told everyone. She would have paraded it around like she did that silly T-shirt she won in an art contest when she was a freshman.

If Dad gave her my bracelet, he did it on purpose. He gave her that bracelet knowing I would see it. He gave her that bracelet knowing when I saw it, I'd be hurt. He wanted to rub it in. He wanted to remind me that I was the ungrateful bitch who didn't deserve nice things.

I had to confront her about it. Face-to-face. It was the only way I could move on. For a brief second, I entertained the idea that she had stolen it. The thought calmed me, and the more I thought about it, the more I accepted it. But still. I needed to ask her to her face so I could watch her eyes and body language.

Because Dad was in a good mood, and I didn't know how long it would last, I didn't bother asking if I could hang out with Eden at her house. Monday morning, we had a huge chemistry test, so it was the perfect lie to invite her over. We'd been so busy prepping for the invitational that we had neglected our homework, and since I wasn't allowed to get bad grades, he'd believe that lie. Since he was so busy working on his speech, he wouldn't even notice she was here.

When Rachel walked by, I hit the mute button on the remote. "Can you ask Dad if I can invite Eden over?"

"He's kind of busy right now."

"We have a chemistry test on Monday. We'll stay out of the way. Promise."

She sighed heavily, like asking a simple question was such a burden for her. "I'll try. In the meantime, straighten up the house a bit. I know you're crashing right now, but if he sees you tidying up, he might okay it."

"Fine. I have laundry to do anyway."

While Rachel worked on my father, I cleaned my room and put a load of clothes in the washer. I even cleaned the kitchen to prove I could be a good little girl.

About a half an hour later, Rachel came in to make a fresh pot of coffee. "He said it's okay, but he doesn't want you leaving the house."

My back to her, I rolled my eyes. Whatever. I dropped everything and called Eden.

"Hey. Want to come over and study for Chem?"

"Sure," Eden said, without hesitating. "I'm bored out of my mind."

"I know, right? Do you have the car?"

"I do, actually, but I have to be back around six. Mom has to go to work"

"Okay. See you in a few."

"Is she coming?" Rachel said, abruptly.

I jumped, not realizing she was still behind me. "For a little while. Her mom needs the car later."

"What's her mother like?"

"She's okay, I guess. Smokes a lot. Works a lot. Babies Eden."

"Mothers do that."

I bit my tongue. "Can I break open the tube of chocolate chip cookies?"

"I forgot that was in there. That would go perfect with my coffee. Don't eat all of them."

"We'll try to save you some."

"Rachel, are you done out there yet?" My dad called out from his office.

Perfect timing. Something about sharing a potential bonding moment with Rachel squiffed me out. It was one thing to bond over the shit Dad dished out. It was another thing entirely to start getting all touchy-feely about cookies and mothers. Don't get me wrong. I liked Rachel more when my father was in a good mood. She was a totally different person, but that didn't mean I wanted her to start being all maternal and shit, especially with my mom back in my life. Still, I could do without her altogether.

The doorbell rang the same time the oven timer went off. I silenced the beeping and raced to the front door before Eden rang the bell again. "Hey, come on in. I have to get the cookies before they burn."

"I hope you didn't bake those on my account."

"It was Rachel's idea. She wants some to eat with her coffee."

"Sounds cozy."

"Take your coat off and get comfortable." As Eden took her jacket off, I kept an eye on her left wrist. She wore a baggy short-sleeved T-shirt but no bracelet. She wasn't wearing any jewelry other than her earrings. Of course, she wouldn't wear the bracelet to my house. That would be too obvious. "Hungry?"

"Nah, I'm good. My tummy's a little yucky today."

I slipped my hand into an oven mitt and opened the door, fanning the heat wafting out, and eyeballing the cookies before placing the cookie sheet down on the stove top. "What's wrong?"

She dropped her bag to the floor by the door. "Probably from all the running we've been doing."

"I get that way sometimes. I have pretzels and ginger ale or hot tea and toast if it's that bad."

"Pretzels and ginger ale sound good."

As I crossed the kitchen to the pantry for the pretzels, my father darted out of his office, his eyes focused over my shoulder. I might as well not have been there. "Eden, how are you?"

She smiled and pushed her hair behind her ear. "Good, how are you?"

"I'm fantastic. Come on in."

She smoothed the fabric of her T-shirt. "Bit of a mess today."

"Ah, don't worry about it. Look at me."

My father wore khakis and a polo shirt, ironed crisp and clean, crease sharp enough to cut through cold butter. Even on his days off, he made an effort.

"But you always look good." Eden blushed.

Rachel sneaked up behind me, standing close enough I could feel her breath on me.

"So, you've come to study with my daughter, eh?" His smile was big and natural, unlike the usual show he put on when he talked with someone he had no interest in, which was usually everyone.

"Big chemistry test on Monday."

"I'm sure you'll do fine."

I started to move toward them, to pull Eden away before my dad monopolized the conversation, but Rachel grabbed the tail of my shirt and held me back. I turned toward her slightly, wondering what was up.

"Just watch," she whispered.

"Why?" I mumbled.

"You'll see."

I turned my attention back to Eden. She tilted her head back and forth, gazing up at my dad, batting her eyelashes. He faced her full-on. His feet weren't pointing toward the door, and he wasn't looking for an escape route. There was a look in his eyes that I had seen before.

When I was a kid, I had met a few of his mistresses, although I didn't know it at the time. He looked at Eden the same way he looked at them: hungry, attentive, interested. There were the sideward glances and secret smiles they tried to mask. The distance between the two of them was like a couple slow dancing without touching each other. If I hadn't seen it happen enough, I wouldn't have recognized what was going on right in front of me.

This wasn't a one-sided flirtation, either. There was a give and take going on. Rachel saw it, and she wanted me to see it. We stood side-by-side and watched the Michael Pierce and Eden Rhodes show. My father told dumb jokes; Eden giggled at them. My father nudged her with his arm; she poked him with her finger. Heat inched its way across my chest and up my neck until my face felt hot enough to break a sweat.

"Michael," Rachel said, firmly. He turned, startled. "We have to get back to your speech."

"Yes, yes, yes. The speech. I've been nominated for an award."

"Exciting!" Eden said.

"You should come to the dinner with my daughter."

Rachel rushed to his side and took him by the elbow. "I'm sure she has more important things to do. Let's get this done or you won't even want to go to your own dinner."

"Nice seeing you again, Eden."

"You, too, Mich—Mr. Pierce." She glanced at me, sighed, and raised her eyebrows. "Chemistry, anyone?"

It was hard finding words, but I managed to spit something out. "Let's do this."

"At the table or upstairs in your room?"

"We better go upstairs." I wanted her as far away from my father as possible. "You go up while I grab the snacks."

"Need help?"

"Nah. I got it."

In the kitchen, I took a few deep breaths to calm myself. It didn't work, so I paced the floor, shaking my hands furiously. My father and Eden flirting? This wasn't supposed to happen. She was supposed to irritate him, get under his skin because he didn't like people like her. He warned me about girls like her. She was supposed to be my partner in crime while we looked for our parents together. She was supposed to be my friend, not his. I wanted to barf. The bracelet, God, the bracelet. She didn't steal that bracelet. He gave it to her, and she took it!

Nine

Over the next two weeks, I tried to distance myself from Eden. Knowing she was wearing my bracelet on her wrist irritated me to no end. Knowing who gave it to her made me rage inside. But the more I resisted her, the more she ended up at my house after school. I couldn't seem to say no to her. My father managed to be at home on the days she was there. At first I thought, oh, that's a coincidence, but by the third time, it became less of a coincidence.

While Eden was there, Rachel kept a close eye on her and never left my father's side. She never let him get too close to Eden, and he hated it. He'd throw his hands up in the air and storm off to his office, yelling something about not having any room to breathe in his own house.

One day, when I had to drive Eden home, Dad chased after us as we headed to my car.

"Eden. Christa," my father said, out of breath. "How would you like to come to the university? I can give you a tour."

Eden's eyes lit up. "That sounds like fun."

"Michael," Rachel called from the house. "Your phone is ringing."

"I've been waiting for this call. Anyway, think about it. Let me know." He dashed off to the house, waving over his shoulder. Rachel stood in the doorway after he passed and glowered at me. This gave me an idea.

Dad never invited me to his office before. Ever. In fact, he discouraged me from ever coming to campus without his permission now that I had my own car, but Eden didn't know this.

"I don't want to go," I said, faking resistance.

"Please." She tugged on my arm like a little kid begging a parent to buy a box of sugary cereal.

"Why do you want to go so badly?" Of course I knew she wanted a chance to spend some time with my dad, away from the eagle eyes of his wife. "It's only a university filled with students."

"Exactly! Think of all the cute guys."

I hadn't thought of that, so I tried to play it off. "Guys who aren't interested in high school girls."

She rolled her eyes and threw her bag in the backseat. "You don't know anything, do you?"

"I guess not. Educate me."

"Some of those college boys are only eighteen-years-old. That's not much of an age difference, so why wouldn't they be interested in us?"

"Because we're still in high school."

"Come on. Don't you just want to shake things up and do something naughty? Unclench those ass-cheeks of yours for once."

"Excuse me?"

"I'm just joking. Sheesh."

Since we were on this track, I thought I'd run it out a little more, see what buttons I could push. "What about Kyle?"

She kicked at the back tire of my car. "He's a jerk."

"So, you're trolling for an older boyfriend?" *Like my Dad?*

"Hello, we're graduating next year."

She didn't take the bait. "I don't want to be around my Dad any more than I have to, okay?"

Her cheeks turned pink. "Why? He's cool."

"To you, maybe."

"I heard there's a really cool coffee shop at the student union. We can get a latte and hang out. We don't have to chill with your father."

"You can get a latte anywhere."

"But I bet they taste better at college."

"Are you serious?"

Eden sighed. "You really need to lighten up. When you go away to college, you're going to be a wild woman. Just watch."

I played with her long enough, especially after the *lighten up* comment. I've heard it before, usually from Janel, but hearing it come out of Eden's mouth pissed me off. "Fine. We'll get a latte and hang out."

Since the invitation was there, I decided to make the most of it. I wanted to see for myself, not through Rachel's jealous lens, just how far these two had gone.

After school on a Thursday afternoon, Eden and I drove to the university to visit my father. We were going to hang out and pretend we were students. By the next fall semester, at my dad's insistence, I'd be walking on that campus, not pretending.

"Do you have a special parking pass?"

I gazed up at the storm clouds moving in. "No, only my father has one, but he wouldn't let me use it even if I wanted to."

"Why not? My father would do that for me."

"Well, your father sounds like a nice guy."

Eden's smile could have lit up the night sky. "He is."

Rain drops dotted the windshield. "It's starting to sprinkle. If we run over, we can make it in no time."

"I'm not running. Don't you have an umbrella?" Eden touched up her makeup in the sun visor mirror. And then it occurred to me, she was fully made up like she was going on a date: eyeliner, eyeshadow, blush, lip gloss, mini-skirt, and heels.

"Probably in the trunk. Aren't you cold dressed like that?"

"Not at all. Ready?"

As we walked through the quad to get to my father's office, guys practically tripped over themselves to get a look at Eden. They certainly weren't checking me out. I wore skinny jeans and a baggy sweatshirt with running shoes.

Eden giggled and waved at the guys. "See, I told you."

All the attention made me want to put a blanket over me.

My father's office was on the second floor of one of the older buildings on campus. Every time I walked inside, I inhaled deeply. It was a good smell of old wood and old books. It smelled the same in the library. I hadn't been on campus in a long time, but the smell brought back so many memories. Like the time I hid in the stacks at the library when I was five years old. My father and Rachel went nuts looking for me. It was the first time I had gotten the belt, but it was worth it.

"Hello, Christa," said Thelma Stone, my father's secretary. She was getting ready to leave. "The last time I saw you, you were probably a foot shorter. I can't believe how much you've grown." Thelma always gave me a lollipop from her secret stash when I came to visit. She told me it was a special treat for a special girl. Those were the good old days. "You look so much like your father."

I gritted my teeth at the comment. "How are you doing?"

"Running a little behind, but life is good. I have to pick up my son. He sprained his ankle in football practice, so if you'll excuse me. It was nice seeing you again."

"You, too."

Eden stared up at the portrait-covered walls of the outer office. "So, this is where your father works. It smells very academic."

I actually laughed out loud in close proximity to my father, something I never did freely.

"Dr. Michael Pierce. I didn't know he was a doctor," she said, pointing at the name plate on the door.

"Ph.D., not a medical doctor."

"Well, duh! I'm not stupid. Still cool, though."

"Eden? Is that you?" My father's voice boomed from behind his door. He jerked it open, smiling like a fool. Until he saw I was there, too. "Oh, hey."

Just out of normal reaction, my body tensed. "Hi, Daddy. I came to show—"

"I see you've made it, Eden."

And just like that, I became invisible.

"Let me give you a little tour."

He pointed to the pictures of the old deans and explained their contribution to the school. I never got this tour. I didn't know who any of those guys were sitting in those pictures. My father whispered to Eden how nice she looked. She blushed and looked away, holding her hands behind her back. I wanted to scream. Instead, I had an idea on how I could spy on them.

"Dad, can I use your office phone?"

"What's wrong with your cell?"

"I thought I charged it last night, but the battery's dead. I need to make a call before it gets too late."

He grumbled. "Go ahead."

The original plan was for Eden and me to hang out at the coffee shop in the student union, but I doubted she'd be too upset if I left her alone with Dad. "Do you want me to run over to the coffee shop and get us something to drink?"

The two of them said that was a good idea and told me what they wanted. I tried to keep them talking so they couldn't hear what I was doing in the office. I set the ringtone on my cell to vibrate before dialing my number from my father's desk phone. The battery wasn't dead at all. I answered the call and carefully placed the desk phone back on the base without hanging up and disconnecting the call.

"I'll be back in a few minutes," I said, rushing out the door.

I walked down the stairs with my cell pressed to my ear and waited for my father and Eden to start talking. I wanted to know what they talked about. Were they discussing me and how I ran off to find my mother? What did they have to say to each other?

I heard his office door shut. "We only have a few minutes," my father said, breathless.

"What if we get caught?"

"Everyone's gone for the day, and I can't handle the way you look right now. You're driving me crazy. Do you have any idea what you do to me?"

I nearly tripped down the steps. I held onto the railing so I wouldn't collapse to the floor.

"Show me," Eden said.

In a matter of seconds, I heard moaning and heavy breathing coming out of my phone. I pulled it away from my ear, wanting to hurl it at the wall. My gut twisted in knots, churning up a sour taste in my mouth. This was more than an innocent flirtation. They were fucking. I couldn't listen any longer and ended the call.

I sprinted across campus, up the steps of the student union, and straight to the bathroom. I locked myself in a stall and sank to the floor. Sucking in short, shallow breaths, my head spun. The room grew dark, then light, then dark again. Running taught me how to control my breathing, but this time I couldn't right it so easily. If I didn't get it back to normal quickly, I'd pass out. I closed my eyes and took a deep breath and held it for seven seconds before releasing it slow and steady. After a minute of that, I felt better, but my brain was still reeling.

What happened back there? I wasn't prepared for what I heard even if I had set them up and gave them the perfect opportunity to do exactly that. By the sound of it, they had done this before. What a punch to the gut. I knew Dad chased after women, but this…this was disgusting.

Something in my head clicked. Like I actually heard the noise. It was so loud my body responded. I felt it, physically. I stopped shaking in an instant. I knew what I was going to do, what I had to do. I would walk out of this bathroom stall, pick up the coffee, and go back to my father's office like I hadn't heard a thing. Pretending I didn't know my father was secretly hooking up with my best friend wouldn't be that hard. It was just another bruise to conceal. While I let this revelation simmer under the surface, I would plan and plot. This was too good not to use against him.

The food court in the student union was mostly empty. A few students sat at tables with books and notebooks open, a coffee cup within reach, and earbuds snuggled in place. Smells of pizza and greasy things made me gag. I swallowed hard. "Two cappuccinos and one caramel latte, please."

"You look familiar." A girl with a nose ring and way too much eyeliner studied me as she filled my drink order. "What's your major? I think I've seen you in one of my classes."

"My father is Dr. Michael Pierce. You might've seen him around." Saying his name out loud made me want to punch a wall. "Maybe you slept with him."

She jerked her head backwards. "Excuse me?"

"I said maybe you met him. He's the Dean of Liberal Arts."

She put her hand over her chest and laughed. "Oh my God, I thought you said I slept with him."

"No, no, why would I say something like that? That would be creepy, right?"

"Especially since I like chicks."

My cheeks burned. "Sorry. Everyone tells me I look exactly like my father, so that's probably why I look familiar to you. I'm sure you've seen him around campus."

"Do you want whipped cream on the caramel latte?"

I nodded.

"I'm a liberal arts major so anything's possible. Can I get you anything else?"

"I'm good, thanks. See you around."

When I opened the door to the building of my father's office, the smell I once liked so much hit me in a new way. It changed from being comforting to something that stank as bad as a decaying carcass. Was there anything he touched that wasn't eventually ruined for me?

Outside the office, I took a deep breath and smiled before stumbling through the door like nothing was wrong. Because nothing was wrong. Yet.

"There you are." Eden rubbed her hands together and reached for the latte. "We were wondering what happened to you."

"There was a line out the door."

Dad took his drink. "You left my phone off the hook."

I froze. Hopefully, with my father's sex fueled brain, he didn't think to push redial because my cell number would have shown up on the display. "Oh. I guess I was in a hurry to get the coffee. I'm out of practice using a landline. I mean, who uses those things anymore?"

"Old people." Eden laughed.

Dad's face turned red. He hated to be reminded of his age, especially coming from the young girl he'd just screwed. Eden probably didn't even realize what she'd said, but I enjoyed the dig.

"I'm ready when you are. I've got a paper to write." I didn't really, but I couldn't stand looking at that man's face any longer.

"Can you drop me off at my house?"

My father watched Eden's every move. He looked like a hungry animal wanting to go back for a second helping of his prey. He never bothered to look at me, and I stood less than ten feet away from him.

"Tell Rachel I'll be home a little later. I've got some things to wrap up for the banquet this weekend."

"I'll be sure and tell her exactly what you're doing."

He smiled with that fake, toothy grin of his, not an ounce of guilt or shame registering on his greedy face. "Thanks for stopping by. I hope you enjoyed the tour, Eden."

"I enjoyed it very much."

The anger I thought I had under control came bubbling to the surface, and so did the cappuccino. I wanted to scream or barf or both. Instead, I dug my nails into the palm of my hand and forced myself to smile.

On the walk across campus, Eden smiled to herself, but she didn't think I noticed.

"You don't talk about Kyle much. I take it by the jerk comment earlier you two aren't dating anymore."

The smile disappeared from her face. "I don't want to be tied down to anyone right now. I want to have fun, and these cute guys on campus are so yummy."

"Like my father?"

It started to rain a little. Then it rained harder, yet Eden didn't bother to answer my question. She took her heels off and ran to the car, splashing puddle water all over her bare legs. I walked casually, not caring if I got drenched. I had the key fob, and I didn't unlock the door until I got to the car.

By the time I made it to the car, we were both soaked. Eden's teeth chattered as she dabbed a napkin under her eyes, smearing mascara everywhere, making her look like a raccoon. As the rain pelted the car, my cell vibrated in my pocket.

Eden stared at me questioningly. "I thought you said your phone was dead."

"It wasn't." I smiled.

She made a hmm noise and turned toward the window sharply.

She knew I knew what went on in that office.

Ten

Rachel grabbed me before I headed out the door for school the next day. "Ow! What are you doing?" I jerked out of her clutches and rubbed my wrist. "I'm going to be late."

"Keep your voice down." She gazed up at the ceiling, nervously. My dad was clearly upstairs getting ready for work, but she acted like he could hear her from down in the kitchen. "You're going to come down with the stomach flu tonight and won't be able to go to the awards dinner."

"What's going on?"

"Where's my paisley tie?" Dad yelled.

Rachel jumped. "Just do as I say." She reached in the pocket of her robe, pulled out a small box, and shoved it in my hand. "Keep this where no one will find it."

"What is it?"

"You'll find out soon enough. Now get going."

Dad's footsteps at the top of the stairs ended our conversation. Rachel pushed me out the door. I raced to the car before I got in trouble for already being three minutes behind schedule. It was only three minutes, but it was enough to provoke him.

Before I made it to the stop sign at the end of the block, I pulled over to the curb and opened the box. Inside there was a cheap flip-phone and a handwritten note from my mother. I couldn't believe it. Sneaky Rachel playing mediator for the enemy. I wasn't even going to question the how and why of it all.

I opened the letter and read out loud: "Christa, if everything goes according to plan, I'll stop by Friday night around seven o'clock to see you. Do not tell anyone about this. If these plans fall through, use the cell phone to call me."

As I read the note, my skin tingled. My mother, coming to see me, in my father's house? How rich. This was perfect. What would he say if he came home, drunk as fuck, and found his ex-wife chilling on the couch with his daughter? Maybe I could convince her to stay as late as possible to make that happen.

"My number is programmed in the contact list already. Call me any time you want, but hide the phone someplace where your father can't find it. Put it on vibrate, and don't forget to turn it off at night in case some telemarketer decides to call you out of the blue."

I fumbled my way around the phone until I found her name in the contact list and pushed *Call*.

"Mom? It's me."

"Oh, good, you got the phone."

"Rachel said I needed to play sick tonight, now I understand why."

"All you have to do is roll around on the bed, grab your stomach, moan and groan, run to the bathroom a lot, that sort of thing."

"I'll try my best. He's pretty good at knowing when I'm faking it. I can tell you where to park so you can sneak through the yard just like—"

"Just like his mistresses. I know all about it, thanks to Rachel. Look for me at the back door."

Something about this sneaking around bit made me want to jump out of the car and run around in traffic like an idiot. "I can't wait to see you. Should I do anything special?"

"Just put on a show."

Oh, that was easy. I'd been trained how to do that from the time I was a little girl.

I was humiliated for getting a B on a test, spanked for saying something I shouldn't have, ignored for doing something I didn't know was wrong, slapped because he was in a bad mood, and through it all, I covered it up with a smile and pretended everything was okay. I was still pretending. I spent my whole life believing my mother didn't want me, acting like I didn't care. Just had my ass beaten black and blue because I tracked her down. But, hey, no big deal. I swallowed the pain with a couple of aspirin and kept smiling. What was one more act to perform?

I clutched my stomach and rolled around on the bed, moaning, like my mother suggested. Rachel reached for my forehead as my father ducked in out and of my room in various stages of dress.

"I can't believe this is happening right now." He was probably worried how it was going to look if his only daughter wasn't at the ceremony to support him. What would all the important people think? "What did you eat today?"

"I didn't eat anything." I spoke softly and moaned at the right times. "The girl sitting behind me in AP English threw up in class. She must've been sick or something." I wrapped my arms around a pillow and curled up in a fetal position.

"Does she have a temperature?" My father raised his voice a bit, still not completely angry. To be honest, I was surprised at how calm he was, at how well he was handling it. Maybe he was distracted by the speech he had to deliver.

"She's burning up," Rachel said, feigning concern.

I caked dark blush on my cheeks to make me look flushed and hid a heating pad under the covers to raise my body temperature in case Dad got suspicious and checked for himself.

"Use a thermometer, not your hand."

"We don't have time. It's obvious she's sick, and I still have to get dressed."

"I don't care." My father left the room. I heard him rustling around in the linen closet in the hall. When he came back in covering the tip of the thermometer with one of those little sheaths, Rachel and I exchanged worried glances.

"Let me do it." She took it from him. "Go and get dressed so we're not late."

"I want to see it when I come back in here. If she's not at 101°, she's getting dressed. How much did you pay for that dress anyway?" Now my dad was getting angry because money was involved.

To escape getting my temperature taken, I made a mad dash to the bathroom and pretended to throw up. I had a cup of water sitting in the bathtub to make my stomach flu sound more believable. I groaned for effect, dry heaved a few times, and flushed the toilet. Before I walked out the door, I splashed a little water on my face to make it look like I was sweating. I threw myself down on the bed, moaning even louder.

"Goddammit," my father screamed from his bedroom. "If I didn't know better, I'd swear she was faking it."

"I'll have the neighbor check on her," Rachel said.

"I don't want some stranger in my house."

But hooking up with your mistresses in the bed you shared with your wife is all right?

"They're not strangers to me. Now, don't get yourself worked up before your big speech."

Long pause. "You're right. If she's stupid enough to get sick, then she's on her own as far as I'm concerned. I hope she vomits the rest of the night."

"I can stay home if—"

"Absolutely not. You're my wife, and you'll be there even if you start shitting your guts out."

Normally, I would have been cowering and anticipating some verbal or physical blow when he was in this state, but I wasn't worried. I was amused. This was funny. Watching my father get bent out of shape over losing even a little control was hilarious. He couldn't control my stomach, and he hated not having control. For once, I was the one pulling the strings.

Maybe it was because of the little brain-snap after I heard him and Eden together or because I'd finally met my mother that I cared less and laughed more. It didn't matter how I got to this point; it only mattered that I got here. Still, I had to continue with my performance until they left the house because if I broke character for a second, he'd pull me off the bed and dress me himself.

Every time Dad walked past my room, I writhed in pain and moaned. It seemed to work. He gave up in frustration, giving me his usual acid look that meant I was going to get it later. And I probably would, but I didn't care.

When they finally left, I let out a long sigh of relief. That was the hardest act I ever had to perform. If he had just walked to the side of the bed near the wall and not the hallway, he would have seen the plug to the heating pad, and BOOM, just like that, he'd snatch me up to my feet and make me get dressed. I raced to the bathroom, washed the blush off my face, brushed my teeth, and got myself presentable. I caught myself smiling, feeling a foreign sensation coming from the inside out. I was so used to clenching, stiffening, and worrying about what was going to come next that I had no idea what I was feeling at that moment, waiting for my mother to show up. Happiness? Joy? Excitement? Maybe all of the above? Whatever it was, I liked it.

About twenty minutes after Dad and Rachel left, my cell rang. Eden's name showed up on the screen. Why was she calling? She usually texted. I answered warily, carrying on with the act.

"Eden?" I moaned softly. "What's going on?"

"I just called to see how you're feeling."

I wasn't going to let this one slide. "What do you mean, *how you're feeling*?"

"Well, you know, I thought you might want someone to talk to, that's all." Her stammering gave her away. She was lying.

"You knew I was supposed to go to the ceremony tonight, right?" I made a gagging noise.

"Oh, was that tonight?" Long pause. "You mean you didn't go? Are you sick or something?"

"Stomach flu. Aren't you supposed to be at work?"

"I was on break and thought I'd give you a call. Anyway. Breaks go fast, so I better get going. Call me later?"

"If I feel up to it."

As the display on my cell went dark, I wondered: How did she know I was home? My father probably told her to check up on me. If they were fooling around, they were probably texting or sexting or whatever people did. Normally, she just texts me unless it's really important. Calling me out of the blue like that, right after Dad and Rachel left? Yeah, nothing suspicious about that at all.

I heard a soft knock at the back door. I jumped up and ran but stopped myself in case it was another of my father's spies. Through the curtain, I saw a short person in dark clothes and a hat. I didn't dare turn the porch light on.

Mom threw her arms around me and squeezed me tight. With my face buried in her hair, the smell of her shampoo triggered the memory of the first time I met her. The nervous excitement I felt that day tickled my insides again.

"Get your things, and let's go." She was out of breath and trembling.

"Get my things and go? Why? What are you saying?" I closed the door behind her and shut off the overhead light, so no one could see inside. "You told me to pretend to be sick and that was it. You didn't say anything about packing my clothes and going anywhere."

"I know. We don't have much time, but if we go now, we can get to my sister's in Ohio before Michael even knows you're gone. This is our chance, Christa."

I had dreamed of running away many, many times, but I never did it. I was always afraid because I had no place to run and wouldn't know how to survive on the streets. In school, we read about what happened to young girls when they ran away—if they didn't get raped or killed, they ended up being trafficked. But that wasn't my concern. "I can't. I only have a few more months of school and as much as I want to leave here, I'm not dropping out."

I could see the disappointment in her eyes. "But I thought you wanted to come and live with me."

"I do, but..." If I really wanted to leave, I would have jumped at this chance, but this wasn't part of the plan to destroy my father. Leaving with my mother would complicate things, but I had to make up something quick. "I'm scared."

She gently rested both hands on my shoulders and looked up into my face, her eyes intense. "I know you are. So am I. But we can do this together."

I stepped back slowly and crossed my arms. "Let's talk about this before we do something that'll get us both in trouble."

Reality was setting in for my mom. I could see the shift in her eyes, her facial expression, and her body. Right before my eyes, she deflated. "You're right. I shouldn't have sprung this on you. My sister told me it was a bad idea, that I should get to know you before trying anything like this."

"I can make you a cup of tea."

She fanned her face with her hands, trying to calm herself. "That would be nice."

As I filled the kettle with water and plopped the tea bags in the cups, I thought about how to tell my mother her sister was right. I wanted to be near my mother, or away from my father at the very least, but she was still a stranger to me. "My friend, Eden, just reunited with her father. He left her and her mother when she was seven. They've been emailing back and forth and chatting and getting to know each other again. Slowly. It seems to be working for them."

My mother hung her head and nodded. "I was so desperate to have you back in my life, I never thought how you felt about everything. I can only imagine the lies that man must've told you. It'll probably take some time for you to trust me."

The kettle whistled. "It'll take the rest of my life to clear my head of his poison. For the record, I never believed what he said about you. I mean, when you saw me out on the sidewalk, you knew who I was before you even saw my face. That says a lot."

My mother lay her head in her hands and cried. I gave her a sheet of paper towel.

"I'm a good student. I'll probably be valedictorian. If I want to make a better life for myself, for us, I need to be careful. It's only a few more months, Mom, and once I graduate, I'm leaving here for good. I don't ever want to see that man again as long as I live, but I want to graduate. I love school. I know that makes me a weirdo. The other kids at school tease me about it all the time, but I don't care. It's the one thing in my life that's mine. I'm proud of what I've done. Dad has nothing to do with my grades. Nothing." The second the words came out of my mouth was when I realized the good grades were his, too. He'd stood over me and drilled me in every subject when I was younger. By the time I graduated from elementary school, I was fanatical about homework.

As my mother bobbed her tea bag in the water, I placed the sugar bowl and the half-and-half in front of her.

"You're not saying much. It's kind of strange for me to do all the talking for once."

"I want to hear you talk." She scooped two teaspoons of sugar in her cup and stirred. "It's good to hear your friend has reunited with her father. I hope we can do the same." She shook her head sadly. "I feel like such an idiot."

"Why?"

"I came here thinking you'd just pick up and go with me."

"Don't do that. This isn't your fault or my fault. This is all Dad's doing."

"It hurts to see that you have a life without me. Fifteen years. I missed out on every single bit of it. Even if Rachel was kind enough to send your pictures and keep me updated, I missed out on the day-to-day stuff. I can never get that back, especially in one day."

I sat in the chair next to her. "I'm a planner. I'm one of those weird people who make lists and crosses things off those lists. Believe me, your name is the first thing on that list right after graduation." The more I talked, the more I believed my own words, but it seemed to work on her. She believed me, maybe just hoping for relief after I disappointed her, and I felt less guilty because of it.

105

"What do we do in the meantime?" she said.

"We email. We talk. The cell phone was genius. I'm good at hiding things."

Even if it was a smile of resignation, it was still a smile, and that was when I realized I did get something from my mother.

The moment was quickly interrupted by a strange noise coming from the laundry room just off the mudroom. Mom didn't notice the sound or if she did, she didn't react to it. When the house was this quiet, I knew what noises to expect: the furnace kicking on, the popping of the wood on the deck as it changed from a warm day to a cold night, the garage door—all that stuff. This sound was a thump on the ground.

"Mom, I'll be right back."

I raced upstairs to the guest room directly over the laundry room. The window faced the backyard away from the street light so I didn't expect to see much, but there was a half-moon that cast shadows of trees and bushes across the ground. There was a light that seemed to float in the air but was aimed at the ground, moving toward the woods at the back of the house. Since I didn't believe in the supernatural, I figured it out pretty quickly. Someone was walking through the yard, using the flashlight app on their phone. When my dad told me that someone was always watching me, he wasn't kidding.

Eleven

I decided not to tell my mother about the person in the yard. Why worry her? I tried to convince myself it was probably nothing. For all I knew, it might have been a prowler or a prankster. The stupid kid who lived a couple houses over was getting older and starting to act out, like leaving bags of flaming poop on the porches in the neighborhood or draping toilet paper over the hedges in our yard. Dad loved that one. Deep down, I didn't believe it myself, but maybe fear of getting caught fueled my denial.

As much as I hated to do it, I chased my mother out of the house by ten o'clock. Although, I would have loved to have seen the fireworks when Dad walked in on me and mom drinking tea at the table, I didn't want her to get in trouble. I was sure I was already in enough trouble for faking my stomach flu.

After she left, and to continue with the charade, I grabbed a blanket from the hall closet and curled up on the couch. I placed my mother's mostly empty tea cup and a plate of half-eaten dry toast on the end table. I didn't expect them home until much later, so I took advantage of the freedom and watched old movies until I fell asleep.

They came home around one o'clock in the morning, drunk, stumbling up the stairs to their room, waking me from a deep sleep. I gave them about twenty minutes before checking in on them to make sure they were down for the night. They had collapsed on the bed, still dressed in the clothes they wore for the evening.

Downstairs, I noticed the keys never made it to the key rack, the shoes never made it to the shoe rack, and the coats dangled off a dining room chair. Oh, and look, two cell phones that never made it to the charging station on the kitchen counter. There was my father's phone sitting right in front of me. All I had to do was pick it up and swipe it.

I held his phone under a light, tilting it left and right to find the pattern from the smudges of his fingers. I pressed the pattern of numbers in different combinations until I finally figured out his passcode. It was his birthday. That took all of a minute. Real smart, Dad.

Not sure how safe it was, I hurried through the list of text messages, searching for Eden's name, but there was no sign of it anywhere. There were a shit-ton of messages from his colleagues and friends, congratulating him for the award. I kept scrolling until I finally saw the single letter E. It had to have been her.

Michael: Could you check on Christa? She says she's sick, but I think she's lying.

E: Not comfortable with this.

I smiled as I read that. At least she protested.

Michael: You owe me one, remember?
E: At work. Busy.

Owed her one? What the hell did that mean?

Michael: Do it on your break.
E: Fine, whatevs. But no more.

"Christa!"

Startled at the sound of Rachel's high-pitched voice behind me, I jumped, sending the phone flying out of my hands and crashing to the floor. Lucky for me, it landed on the Oriental rug and not the wood. "What are you doing up?" I struggled to catch my breath.

"If he finds you playing with his phone, you're going to get more than the belt." Rachel rushed to pick it up, inspecting it for damage. "You're lucky it's not broken."

"Please don't say anything to him."

"What were you looking for anyway?"

I wondered if Rachel knew how far her husband had gone with Eden. "Nothing." I said it in a way that was sure to make it sound like I was hiding something, hoping it would cause her to pry even more. She needed to know, but if I came out and told her about the texts, she'd dismiss it, saying that I was doing it to provoke her.

"Don't lie. I may be drunk, but I know when you're lying."

"I'm not lying. Honest."

"How stupid do you think I am?"

"You have the phone in your hand. No one is stopping you from checking it."

She must have been really drunk because it took her a few seconds to realize she was holding the phone the entire time. "But it's his. He'll know."

"He's upstairs. You're down here. I won't tell if you don't."

She tilted her head side-to-side, squinting as she read the messages on her husband's phone. "E? Who's E and why was E checking up..? Oh. E." I could see it hitting her, the realization sobering her up real quick. "Just so I'm not jumping to conclusions, E is Eden, right?"

I nodded.

"How did you figure out his password?"

"It's his birthday. Not very original."

She placed the phone gently on the dining room table next to hers. She was checking out, going to her happy place. I could see it behind her eyes, like a curtain closing. She did that when she didn't want to deal with Dad's affairs.

Considering how much she had a hand in helping my mother, I actually felt badly for her, but if I wanted to carry out my plan, I needed her gone. She was in the way.

"Are they just texting?"

I took a deep breath, not wanting to remember the disgusting sounds I heard coming out of my phone when I spied on them in Dad's office. "It's more than that."

Rachel tried to smile it away as usual, but her face wasn't cooperating this time around—maybe because she was drunk or maybe because she was finally accepting the truth. She grew as pale as the bleached wood of the kitchen cabinets. "Eden?"

"It bothers me just as much as it bothers you."

She braced herself against the table before collapsing into a chair. "I saw the way he looked at her, the way she looked at him. I thought they were just flirting, thought there's no way he'd touch her. That son of a bitch."

I stood next to her, wondering if I should pat her on the head in feigned sympathy or help her pack her bags. "What are you going to do about it?"

"I'm not going to stick around while he fools around with a child, that's for sure. She's a child."

"And my best friend."

Rachel gazed up at me with bloodshot eyes. "You still call her that?"

"Only to her face."

"This is inexcusable. Unforgivable." She attempted to get up but stumbled backwards. "I have to get out of here."

"Where are you going to go?"

"You think I'd tell you that?"

"Why wouldn't you?"

"Because once I'm gone, you won't ever see me again."

"I'm not the enemy here."

"Really?" She sneered. "It doesn't matter now anyway. You better get to bed before he wakes up and catches you."

I sighed. "Well, goodnight, I guess."

"Wait. Do you have any money?"

"No." I lied. I did have some money, but I needed it. When I walked into the foyer toward the stairs, I heard Rachel let go. I sat on a step and watched as her shoulders rose and fell in rapid convulsions, her heavy sobs filling the quiet of the house.

Twelve

Eden began to pull away from me over the next week. My attitude toward her didn't help. Ever since I heard her and my father going at it in his office, I had a hard time looking at her I was so sick about the whole mess. They were texting each other. How freaking twisted was that? My dad texting a high school student. He asked her to spy on me. Even if she did it reluctantly, she still did it.

But the sudden change in Eden didn't seem to have anything to do with me. She was mopey, quit wearing makeup, and half the time looked pale and greenish. During first period French, she often ran out without asking the teacher for a hall pass or anything, and each time she came back to the room, her face was red and splotchy.

I figured it had something to do with Kyle, considering she had called him a jerk the last time I brought his name up. Maybe they were fighting. Maybe they had broken up for good. My curiosity got the better of me, so I broke down and asked if she was okay.

"Just a stomach bug I can't seem to shake."

"Did you eat something bad? I mean, you do work in a restaurant."

She suddenly perked up. "Yeah, yes. A few of the other servers have been sick, too. Maybe the food is bad."

"Go to the doctor to rule out food poisoning."

"If it doesn't clear up." She put her hand over her mouth, closed her eyes, and burped and hiccupped at the same time. "I don't think I can run tomorrow."

I stopped at my locker to check my cell phone for messages from Mom before the next class. "Coach won't let you run in the meet if you don't run during practice."

Eden leaned against the wall, hugging a book to her chest. "That's good, because I feel like shit."

"Go to the school nurse. She might have some answers if you can't afford— I mean, if you don't want to go to the doctor."

"I could try. Tell Mrs. White where I went."

"Text me when you're done."

I expected a text from Eden by the end of biology class to let me know how she was, but it never came, and when I texted her, she didn't respond. Maybe the school nurse thought she was sick enough to go to the emergency room or maybe she went home and crashed.

Before school let out, I called Rachel to let her know I was going to stop by Eden's house to check on her.

"Why should you care how she's feeling?"

"Because if she's messing around with Dad, she's going to need a friend," was what I said because it sounded better than *I need to keep her close because she is the bullet in the gun aimed at Dad.* I wanted to know what was going on with her, why she was isolating herself and acting all weird.

"You're a fool." *Said the woman who won't leave her philandering husband.* "You better be home and ready for dinner before five o'clock. He's in a mood."

"I won't be long. If she's sick, she won't want to hang out anyway."

"All right, but I still don't understand why you even care. I know I don't."

"Then why are you still here?"

She hung up on me. I giggled. Sooner or later she would have to make a decision, and I wanted to be there to help her pack up and move.

Eden's mother answered the door, which was unusual because Mrs. Rhodes was always working and hardly ever home, leaving Eden by herself most of the time.

"Christa," she said, happy to see me. "What can I do for you?"

"How's Eden?"

"She's in bed. I didn't even know she was sick until she came home. I never get to see or talk to my own daughter anymore. This shift work is killing me." Mrs. Rhodes was young, but the cigarettes and late nights were starting to catch up to her. The dark circles and bags under her eyes made her look much older than she was.

"Can I see her?" I asked, not wanting to get into small talk, making myself late to get home.

"Knock first to see if she's awake. If she isn't, let her sleep. She looks worn out, poor thing."

I didn't knock before walking in because I was going in no matter what. Eden was awake and crying. "Are you all right? What did the nurse say?" I stuck close to the door, afraid I might catch whatever she had in case it was contagious.

"She said go home, sleep it off, and call the doctor, like I knew she was going to say."

"But why are you crying? I mean, are you in pain?"

"No." She stared off at something behind me before looking at me. "I'm a big baby when I get sick, that's all. It scares me."

"Do you think it's something serious?"

She grew quiet again. Something wasn't right but I didn't know what. It felt like I had walked in on a private conversation. Knowing that Eden had lied to me so many times before, I sensed she was doing it then and was doing it to get rid of me. She knew what was wrong, but she wasn't going to tell me. Yet.

"Did you call the doctor?"

She nodded.

"And?"

"I'm not up to talking right now, so you should go." She fluffed a pillow and pulled a blanket over her shoulders.

"Okay. Call me later if you feel up to it."

She moaned as I closed the door behind me. Her mother stood in the hallway, hands in her pockets, back against the wall. That must have been what Eden was staring at earlier and the reason she didn't want to talk openly. Maybe she really wanted to tell me what was wrong but didn't feel comfortable in front of her mom.

"Is she going to be okay?" I said.

"She'll be fine. We have an appointment tomorrow."

"I hope it's nothing."

"I'm sure it isn't. She's always had tummy issues especially during her period." Mrs. Rhodes smiled and escorted me out of the house. "Thanks for stopping by. I'm sure it made her feel better."

I left Eden's feeling rejected, like I was purposely being left out on some big secret, but when I checked the time on my cell, I forgot all about it because I had something bigger to worry about.

I made it home five minutes before five o'clock and raced upstairs to get ready for dinner. Knowing my father was in a mood, I had to be invisible in case the reason for his mood was my mother's visit when he was at the awards ceremony. I anticipated a blow-up any second.

He kept his head down during dinner, focusing on his food instead of forcing all of us to talk about him and his day. Rachel and I stole glances at each other, wondering what was going on. He didn't demand for anyone to ask how his day was or dominate the conversation. The most he said was "thank you" and a couple of grunts of recognition for the meal Rachel cooked. As soon as he cleaned his plate, he left the table and sat in his chair to watch the evening news.

I helped Rachel clean up the dinner dishes. Since I pissed her off earlier, I thought this was a good way to make up for it, but really I only wanted to pump her for information.

"Does he know?" I whispered.

"Know what?"

"You know." I mouthed the words, my mother.

"I don't think so. Something must've happened at work." She made a slashing gesture across her throat as my father walked into the kitchen.

"I'm going out." Dad grabbed his phone and car keys and walked out the door before we had a chance to say anything, even goodbye.

Actually, his leaving was a relief because it meant Rachel and I could talk. "So, what's going on?"

"I don't know. He started acting this way last night. This morning he was an absolute grump."

"And you're sure he doesn't know about Mom stopping by?" I hadn't told anyone I had seen someone creeping in the backyard, so even if she kept reassuring me that Dad didn't know, I didn't allow myself to trust her word.

"I'm pretty sure, but if you want him to find out keep bringing it up."

"Good point. I'll be upstairs in my room, studying."

Calling my mother was more like it since my father was out of the house. Mom was pretty responsive and usually texted back right away. Most of the time she was busy teaching, so we had to steal moments. It was fun. It felt wrong and rebellious, and I liked it, but that day, she hadn't returned my three texts. That wasn't like her. I called and waited for her to pick up, but she didn't, so I left a voicemail.

My skin prickled as I remembered the shadow lurking in my backyard on the night she came to visit me. I didn't tell my mother someone might have been spying on the house because I didn't think it was important enough to worry her. I figured I was the one who had to worry. I thought for sure I was going to catch hell from my father because he knew I had faked stomach flu so I could hang out with her, but if he knew, he never let on and Rachel assured me he didn't know.

I had a sinking feeling in my gut. Something wasn't right. Something felt off. What if something happened to her again because she came to see me and I didn't tell her about the person in the yard?

Halfway through the next day, I still hadn't heard from my mother. Not only was I scared that something might have happened to her instead of me, I also felt responsible. I should have warned her. At least she would have been prepared, taken precautions.

If something had happened to her, I had no way of knowing. Who would know, and who would I ask? The only person who would know was the lady I met at the coffee shop. If worse came to worse, I could always call and ask her, except I didn't remember her name.

I still had gym class to get through before I could run off to check my email. That day we were playing volleyball, which was good because I had a lot of aggression building up inside me. Playing volleyball gave me a rush. Running didn't do that for me any longer because I was so used to it, but spiking the ball in some girl's face always felt good. Being tall sometimes had its advantages.

As we changed into our gym clothes, I noticed something strange about Eden, another detail I'd missed earlier. I was so wrapped up in other things, like getting to know my mother, trying to out-dodge my father while planning his ruin, that I missed the obvious signs. The baggy clothes she'd started wearing a few weeks ago weren't so baggy anymore. As she was dressing into her gym clothes, she kept tugging her sweatshirt down, like she was hiding something. When she thought no one was looking, she let her hand slip, and that was when I saw it. Eden had gained weight. Her belly was sticking out a little. She caught me staring and quickly yanked the shirt down.

I was stupid for not seeing the signs when they were all in front of me. She was getting sick all the time. Certain foods made her nauseated. She'd gained weight, especially in her boobs. She covered up her growing belly. That was why she didn't want to run anymore, because she couldn't. Eden was pregnant.

And she was fucking my father.

My mind raced back to the day I had heard them together in his office. The room started spinning. Everything around me stopped except one thought. My best friend was carrying my father's baby. That would explain his mood last night. He knew. He knew he got a young girl pregnant. She must have told him, and he had a responsibility to own up to. How was he going to tell his wife, his daughter? What was my father going to do with another kid? He didn't even like the one he had.

"Are you ready to go upstairs?" Eden asked, so innocent and pure.

My mouth moved, but nothing came out. I couldn't even bring myself to look at her. What was I supposed to say to her now that I knew this? What was I supposed to feel after discovering this? She had been hiding it from me for a while now, but there she was standing before me with a baby bump.

She snapped her fingers in front of my face. "Christa, are you ready to go upstairs? It's volleyball. It's time to get back at the fakers."

"Yeah, let's get back at the fakers." Somehow, I managed to stand up, close the locker, and twist the combination lock. I managed to walk upstairs to the gymnasium right alongside Eden, who was pregnant with my father's baby. This changed everything.

During lunch period, I ran off to the computer lab. The last email my mother sent was from two days ago. It was a short one. "Hello, I can't wait to see you again" — that sort of thing. I searched the news for where my mother lived to see if maybe something had happened to her.

There was an incident in her neighborhood. *Woman Hospitalized After Home Invasion.* I scanned the article quickly, mumbling please don't let it be her. *Elizabeth Pierce hospitalized after break-in.* My chest fluttered when I read about what had happened to her. That explained why she hadn't responded to my texts or voicemails. I searched the number for the hospital in her area, ran to the girl's bathroom, and called before my next class.

"Could you connect me to Elizabeth Pierce's room, please?"

"I'm sorry, but she's not taking any calls unless it's close family."

"This is her daughter."

"Could I have your name, please?"

"Christa Pierce."

"One moment, please."

My hands trembled as I waited. The phone rang about five times before my mother answered.

"Are you all right?" I blurted out.

"Hi, honey. I'm all right, just waiting for the doctor to let me go home."

"What happened?"

She cleared her throat. "I was out with Sydney, my friend from the coffee shop, and got home late. Someone wearing a mask broke in while I was in the shower. The man pushed me into the sink. I hit my head on the corner, and that's how I ended up in the hospital. They kept me overnight for observation, slight concussion, but I'm okay now."

I squeezed my eyes shut. Mom was a petite thing. The thought of some big dude knocking her around made me want to punch something. "Did you get a good look at him?"

"I spoke with the police and told them what I could, but without a face, there's nothing they can do."

A rush of heat scrambled across every inch of my body. "I have to tell you something." My stomach twisted in knots when I thought that I could have prevented this. "I know you're going to be mad at me."

"What, honey?" Her sweet voice sounded so confident that no matter what I said, she wasn't going to be angry.

"The night you came to see me, I heard a noise outside near the laundry room."

"The thumping noise?" she said, confused.

"So you did hear it. Anyway, I went upstairs and looked out the window. Someone was walking through the yard, away from the house, using their cell phone for a flashlight."

"I'm not surprised. The guy who broke in told me to keep my distance or else. What else am I supposed to gather from that?"

"That Dad had something to do with this."

She grew quiet.

"I'm sorry," I said, breaking the silence.

"I'm not."

"Maybe that's why he's been acting funny lately." The warning bell rang, and I didn't want to have to explain why I was late for class. "I have to go now. Are you going to be all right?" I headed toward the door.

"Yes, but I'll be staying with Sydney. I don't feel safe being by myself anymore. I know you don't want to go with me yet, but I'm going to Ohio to live with my sister until you graduate. I'm tired of looking over my shoulder, waiting for him to show up and hurt me for good. You understand, don't you?"

"Of course. I couldn't live with myself if he hurt you because of me. But why does he keep doing this to you?"

"He knows he's losing control because you're growing up, and that scares him."

"Christa Pierce." It was the principal, and he was walking behind me. "You better hurry up and get to class."

"I have to go. If I get in trouble at school, Dad will wonder why. I'll talk to you later."

"I love you, Christa."

I stopped cold. I had never heard those words from anyone before in my life. "I love you, too, Mom." I snapped the phone shut and ran the rest of the way to class, feeling something I had never felt before: happiness.

The feeling didn't last long, though. As I sat in class listening to the lecture, my mind drifted away to what had happened to my mother. My father was an unbelievable monster who intimidated people with his position, money, and power. He didn't care about anybody but himself. As long as his lusts were satisfied and he had control, everything was right with the world. For him. He destroyed anything and everyone in his path and expected respect and admiration in return. Those days were over.

Then there was Eden. My so-called friend. I heard them having sex and now she was pregnant. How much longer could he get away with all this? This was the last straw. I was going to put a stop to his reign of terror, and I knew just how to do it. I wanted him to suffer for the rest of his life.

Thirteen

Now that I knew the passcode to my father's phone, sneaking downstairs to check his messages became a nightly ritual. It was the only way I could dig into his life and gather dirt without him knowing about it.

There were cryptic exchanges with someone named David. The last message from my father told this David guy to get away for a while until things calmed down. Dad was dumb enough to leave a digital trail of the whole exchange. Dad always thought he was special, untouchable. The rules didn't apply to him, so I guess it made sense that he'd think he could do something like ordering a man to assault a woman and get away with it.

I also learned that Eden broke it off with him right after he asked her to spy on me. She didn't give a good reason, but I had a feeling it had something to do with her being pregnant. That didn't stop him from messaging her and begging her to come back for more fun, sometimes using the most explicit language. She rejected him with simple statements like busy with work, on my period, not feeling well. So pathetic. He didn't take the hint so she finally told him she didn't want to see him anymore. What amazed me was how careless both of them were, leaving evidence of their relationship. Eden I could understand. Dad, on the other hand, was the adult and should have known better, but then I'd think back to all the news reports of men, even politicians, sending dick pics to women. I could use this to my advantage later on.

One day, a few days into my snooping through his phone, Dad came home early from work with a wild look in his eye. His face was all red and blotchy and sweaty. I turned inward and braced myself for what was to come. Rachel stared at me, confused. I had a feeling this day was going to arrive.

Part of me didn't give a shit if I got caught reading his messages while I was doing it, but seeing him in a rage, I cared. It bothered me how much I cared. Memories of the slap across the face that knocked me into the table after he found out I had visited my mother made me tense up. Phantom sensations of the belt hitting my backside made my bladder want to explode. I was always on edge, anticipating a blow or a raised voice or an insult, but most of those were surprise attacks. Seeing the anger in his face, feeling the rage of energy in the room, remembering the pain that lingered for days after an encounter made me wish I had never touched his phone.

"In the living room. Now." He snapped his fingers and pointed to the couch. "Sit."

We did as we were told, because we knew better.

"Which one of you hacked into my phone?"

I flinched, hoping he didn't notice the movement.

"What are you talking about?" Rachel barely got the words out of her mouth before he yanked her off the couch and pinned her against the wall.

"The dumb act got old long ago. Haven't you learned that by now?"

"Leave her alone." I was surprised by the sound of my own voice. So was Dad.

He let go of Rachel and turned on me. "What did you say?"

The air went out of the room, and for a minute, I thought I was going to pass out. I struggled to take a breath, to stay in the moment. What did I think I was doing? Another word or move and I'd get it, but the audible click in my brain I experienced after hearing Eden and my dad going at it in his office happened again. Everything in the room came back into focus. I saw him. I faced the rage in his eyes. I saw his hand in the air, ready to swing, but I couldn't stop myself. "I said, leave her alone."

"What makes you think you can talk to me like this?"

"What makes you think you can keep terrorizing us like this?"

"Christa, don't get involved." Rachel rubbed her arm where my father grabbed her. As he lunged toward me, she stepped in his way and blocked him. She put her arms on my shoulders and pushed me toward the stairs.

"I'm not going upstairs."

"So, it *was* you who was searching through my phone?" My father came toward me, his fists clenched, his eyes narrowed.

My knees were about to give out at any second. I stood on the bottom step with my hand gripping the railing for support. "I don't know what you're talking about. Why would I go through your phone?"

"That's what I'm trying to find out."

My cheeks clenched, fighting the urge to wet myself. "I wouldn't know how to hack into your phone, and I doubt Rachel would either."

My father took another step closer. The veins in his neck and forehead were popping out. "Maybe the two of you are in it together."

"Why would we do that?" Rachel said, backing away.

"I don't know, you tell me."

"Why don't you tell us exactly what's going on, and then maybe we can help you." Rachel stumbled over her words as she tried to sound confident. "Your yelling isn't helping. You're upset. Let's calm down and talk about this."

"I will not calm down. Someone checked my text messages before I could get to them and I've missed some very important business dealings because of this."

"Maybe you checked them and don't remember," I said. "You've been doing a lot of strange things lately."

Dad narrowed his eyes. "Like what?"

"Just little things." I had to think fast. Usually, I could pull something out of nowhere and make it sound convincing, but with him standing there and staring at me with those intense eyes of his, I found it harder to lie. "Like, I don't know, you left your car keys in the powder room a few times."

"When?"

"You don't remember? That's not good."

"When did I do this, Christa?"

Rachel stood behind my dad, shaking her head slowly. I was screwing this up. I wasn't as good at gaslighting as he was. "I found them on the sink a couple of days ago and put them back on the key rack."

"Quit trying to change the subject."

"I'm not. You've just been forgetful lately, that's all." I should have kept my mouth shut. I should have kept my hand on the railing, because his slap nearly knocked me over, but I caught myself on the hall table.

Rachel screamed.

"Shut up or you're next." He grabbed his keys and left.

Rachel rushed over to me. "Are you all right? Let me get some ice."

I laughed. "Don't bother." In spite of the stinging burn on my cheek, I was proud of myself for standing up to him. I laughed harder. Judging by the expression on Rachel's face, this unnerved her. "If you don't leave right now, you're never going to get out of here." I couldn't have been any more matter-of-fact with her. She had to go. I needed her gone.

She pulled her shoulders back and cleared her throat. I saw something happen behind her eyes again, but instead of a curtain closing, a light went on. She finally got it. "You're right."

I went to my room, dug out the phone, and texted my mother. I told her what had happened and to be on the lookout for trouble. She texted back saying she was already in Ohio with her sister. In an instant, I regretted not going with her when she offered. I could have been in Ohio with someone who loved me instead of feeling the sting of my father's hand on my face again.

While my mother and I exchanged messages, Rachel got in her car and drove away. She didn't even say goodbye. Boo. Hoo.

As soon as she left, I ran to my father's closet and stole a pink button-down Oxford with his monogram stitched on the pocket. MJP. Michael James Pierce. With Rachel gone, there was nothing standing in my way of bringing him down.

Around midnight, he came home.

"Rachel?" He sounded confused, hinging on frantic. He called her name again as he went up the stairs and again when he went into their bedroom. When it finally hit him that she was gone, he knocked on my door.

I pretended to be asleep. He shook my shoulder. "Hey, what's...Dad? What's going on?"

"Where did Rachel go?"

"What do you mean? Isn't she in bed?"

He grabbed the collar of my shirt and pulled me close to his face. "Don't mess with me." His breath smelled of alcohol. "Where did Rachel go?"

"I'm not messing with you. She was here when I went to bed."

He let go of my collar and ran his fingers through his hair. "She's gone. What did you say to her after I left?"

Always trying to blame someone else for something he had done. "Nothing. She asked if I wanted ice for my face. I said no and came upstairs. That was the last time I talked to her." He sobered instantly, it seemed, and stared at the wall for a few seconds. He groaned a few times and mumbled something like oh well, before getting up from my bed and stumbling out of the room. A few seconds later, he slammed his bedroom door shut. I lay in bed, laughing.

Fourteen

Dad slept through his alarm. Tired of listening to the ear-piercing beeps, I shut it off for good and left him sprawled out on his bed, still fully dressed, drool all over the pillow. Seeing him in such a vulnerable state made me wonder why I was so afraid of him. We were practically the same height, the same build, but I doubted my fists could inflict as much pain as his.

Before heading off to school, I allowed myself some extra time to screw up my father's day even more. His car was parked all crooked in the garage. He must have been really wasted last night. I crouched down beside the driver's side front tire, unscrewed the valve cap, and pushed my fingernail on the release stem to let the air out. My nail bent, letting only a few puffs out. It would have been so much easier to hammer a rusty nail into the tire, but I doubted Dad even owned a hammer these days. I found a pointy pair of pliers in a small toolbox sitting on a shelf. Those fit perfectly inside the stem. It took some time, but I managed to get most of the air out of the tire, enough that he'd have to change it to the spare.

In my car, I checked the "bruise" on my cheek. Normally, I would have needed to put concealer on the mark he left behind where he slapped me, but I didn't need to this time. My cheek would often be pink with a small bruise where that stupid ring of his always hit, but last night's slap was more of a push than a full assault to my face. Instead of covering the evidence of his rage, I accentuated it with makeup. No more hiding it.

As I walked the hallway to homeroom, no one asked about the mark on my face, but a lot of people stared, especially the teachers. I had a feeling they knew what was going on at home and they'd known for a long time. What could they do? Report a man like my father to child services?

"Whoa, what happened?" Eden said, eyeing the red and purple spot on my cheek.

"That's what happens when you mess with the wrong person."

Her face lost its color. She said nothing, but I could see she understood I was talking about my father.

"I'd invite you over to hang." I pointed to my face. "But as you can see…"

"You helped me out when I needed it, so you can hang at my house. It's only right I return the favor. Maybe you can help me catch up on my homework since I'm falling behind."

"Cool. I'll stop and get some cheeseburgers and fries or something. Does that sound good?"

She shook her head slowly, unsure. "I'll pass, but if you want something, bring it over. We don't have much to eat anyway. I've been drinking a lot of ginger tea. It seems to be settling my stomach."

"I know how you are with food, so I'll ask again before we leave school."

She laughed nervously. "Not today."

Eden's house smelled of ginger. There was a container of water sitting on the counter with a chunk of it soaking at the bottom. She poured herself a glass as soon as she walked in the kitchen. "Want some?"

I held up the cup of soda I'd gotten when I'd ordered a double cheeseburger and fries—my favorite after school meal when I was away from my father. We never went out for fast food, and it was never brought into the house. If we wanted a burger and fries, Rachel made it. "You're not going to get sick if I eat in front of you, are you?"

"No, but those fries sure look good." She sat down at the table and stared at them.

I pushed the cardboard container across the table and raised an eyebrow. She shook her head.

Manners had taught me better than to eat like a pig at a trough, but I threw all that education out the window and dug into the burger. I wanted her to get sick. Double patties, extra cheese, lettuce, mayo, mustard, and a shit ton of ketchup oozed out as I smashed my face in the bun. The goop dripped onto the paper wrapping below with tiny splats. My fingers were coated with grease and red, white, and yellow blobs of

135

wonderfulness. It was the best thing I'd tasted in a long time. It tasted like freedom, and it caught Eden's eye. Sour faced, she watched as I made a mess all over myself. A few times she swallowed hard and cleared her throat. "Am I being gross?"

She took a sip of ginger tea. "Yeah, but don't let me stop you. When was the last time you ate?"

"Lunch. You sure you don't want any fries?"

Long pause. "All right. I haven't had fast-food in a long time, and it smells so good." She shoved the fries in her mouth one right after another, closing her eyes and moaning in appreciation. "God, these are so freakin' amazing. Do you care if I eat all of them?"

"Help yourself." While she inhaled the fries, I pulled out my anatomy book and pretended I was interested in studying. Sooner or later, that grease would kick in and the pictures of viscera in my book would trigger her gag reflex. She refused to take anatomy because she couldn't handle the yucky stuff.

Eden dug in her bag for her books. "Can I see your notes from chemistry? I missed a couple of classes and need to catch up."

"Just don't get grease on them."

She sucked the grease and salt off her fingers before wiping them on a napkin. "You know, I thought you were mad at me."

That was an understatement. "Why would I be mad at you?"

"I don't know. Paranoid, I guess." She kept her head down but peered up at me with those sad eyes of hers. She squirmed in her chair and let out a small burp. "I always do something wrong." Another burp. Good. The fries were making her sick.

"You okay? You don't look so good."

She put her fist to her mouth and burped again. She closed her eyes, swallowing hard and slow. "I probably shouldn't have eaten that. I haven't eaten anything like that in over a month." She took another gulp of the ginger tea, but before she had a chance to swallow it, she ran off to the bathroom.

I chased after her, pretending to be concerned. "Are you all right?" I didn't need an answer. The gagging and splattering noises were enough. "Do you want me to get you anything?" I called out over my shoulder as I tiptoed down the hall toward her room.

"I'll be out in a second." She turned the ceiling fan on. Perfect. The sound could cover up what I was doing.

While she was in the bathroom being sick, I searched through the jewelry box sitting on her dresser. She had a lot of cheap-looking chains, rings, and bracelets tangled together in clumps, but I found my bracelet at the bottom of the pile. I shoved it in my pants pocket and stepped into the hallway at the same time Eden came out of the bathroom.

"What were you doing in my room?"

"I wasn't in your room. I was pacing back and forth waiting for you to get done, to see if you were all right. So, are you all right?"

She gave me a side-eyed glare. She didn't believe me. I had to smooth this over because I needed her to trust me.

"Are you up for studying?"

She rubbed her belly and moaned. "I'm just going to curl up on the couch and read the chapters I missed."

"I can make copies of my notes for you."

She took a deep breath and let it out sharply. "Looks like you'll be getting valedictorian after all."

"There's still time. Don't give up."

She shook her head sadly. "I don't have much hope lately."

"Did you ever go to the doctor?"

She stared at the floor. "Yeah, but it was some sort of consultation. No diagnosis or anything."

I nodded, not believing a word. "Maybe we can take a drive one day and hang out, just the two of us. Maybe that will make you feel better. Maybe even this weekend."

"I have to work but we can try to squeeze something in."

"Cool. Did I tell you Rachel left?" I watched for her reaction to this bit of gossip.

She turned away from me and headed toward the kitchen. "Do you know why?"

"My father has a little problem with women, if you get my meaning." I had stopped feeling like it was my duty to keep his secrets.

She still couldn't look at me. "I, uh, got that impression about him, but it's none of my business."

"What days do you work this weekend?"

"I close on Saturday night, so I'll be pretty wiped out most of Sunday. My mom and I are doing something Friday night. I'll have to call you."

I tossed my fast food mess in the trash. The smell of grease lingered in the house. "I hope you feel better."

"Sorry you had to drive all the way over here for nothing. I hope I can get back to normal soon."

"Do you talk to Kyle anymore?"

She folded her arms across her chest, making her baby bump more noticeable. "I just spoke with him the other day. He's dating another girl. It sounds serious."

"Does that bother you?"

"Not really. We were never serious anyway."

"You were really excited about him in the beginning."

"You're overly interested in my relationship with Kyle."

"I'm just trying to figure out why you've been so mopey lately."

"Because I don't feel good."

"Look, I can't keep pretending I don't know your secret."

"What secret?"

I paused for dramatic effect. "Are you pregnant?"

Eden's eyes grew big. She jerked her head back and shook her head rapidly. "Where did that come from?"

"I heard rumors."

"Right. Rumors."

"But you've been so sick lately."

She glanced away. "Probably food allergies. My mom and I will figure it out."

It was obvious as the ugly wallpaper in her kitchen that Eden was lying. My face grew hot with anger, but I let her have the lie and changed the subject. "Hey, how's your dad?"

"Good." She perked up every time she got the chance to talk about him. "We're planning my trip to Texas." Her stomach gurgled loudly, and her eyes drooped. "I better go." She ran off to the bathroom, slamming the door shut.

"Okay. I'll see you later." I slipped my fingers in my pocket and felt for the bracelet.

With *my* bracelet back in *my* possession, I started home. I stopped at the drugstore to pick up a pack of latex gloves, paid with cash, and shoved them in my backpack.

My father's car wasn't in the garage. That meant he got the flat tire fixed. There was still no sign of Rachel. Good for her. It took her long enough. Hopefully, she had enough sense to stay away for good or at least long enough to stay out of my way.

With the house empty, I ran to Dad's bathroom and took a couple of his sleeping pills out of the bottle. I couldn't take too many as I was sure he would notice. If he figured out I had hacked into his phone and read his messages, he'd figure out a few of his precious pills were missing.

I ran to the kitchen, grabbed a spoon out of the drawer, crushed the sleeping pills into a fine powder, and scooped it into a small envelope. My pulse quickened. All this sneaking around gave me a rush of energy. I liked it.

An hour later, and he still hadn't come home, so I sneaked into his closet. I found a pair of old pants and boots he used to wear back when he did his own yardwork. He wouldn't notice those missing since he hired a local company to cut the grass now that he had an important image to maintain. His words.

I found an old gym bag stuffed at the back of his closet and took that as well. I stuffed the pants, the boots, and the shirt into the gym bag and buried it at the back of my closet. I took some hair from his hairbrush and put it in a small envelope with the bracelet. That also went into the gym bag.

When I was all finished, I was sweaty and was out of breath. It took me a good half hour to calm down. Once I did, I unpacked my backpack and set up my bedroom like I was doing homework, but I just stared out the window the rest of the night, plotting. If all went well, Dad would be out of my life for good within a week.

Fifteen

After Dad accepted Rachel had left for good, he didn't hang around the house much or talk much. He never asked about the flat tire or even blame me for it. It didn't take me long to figure out he already had someone new in his life. A college student, or so I heard. This was a problem for me. I needed him home.

Saturday morning was the first I had seen him for longer than five minutes, and he was already halfway out the door. I had to run to catch him before he disappeared for the day. "Hold up, Dad."

"I'm in a hurry. What do you need?"

"Should I make dinner tonight?"

"Do you even know how?"

I didn't let the comment get to me. Not this time.

"I could pick up a rotisserie chicken from the store and steam some vegetables. Does that sound good? I mean, I have to eat, too, and with Rachel not around, we don't want to starve."

He flinched at the mention of Rachel's name. "I'm going to the movies right now."

"I'll have dinner waiting for when you get back."

My father always drank a glass of wine in the evening. It was the whole drinking-red-wine-for-health-reasons thing. He wasn't picky about what he drank, so I grabbed a bottle of Merlot from the wine rack. He seemed to have a lot of it, so I assumed it was his favorite. By seven o'clock, I had everything set up, and all I had to do was wait. An hour later, he finally came home.

Not that I cared, but I asked anyway. "How was the movie?"

"Dumb, but it wasn't my choice."

"Everything is ready if you're hungry."

He went to the kitchen and snooped around at what I had prepared. He actually gave a nod of approval but not directly to me so I could see it. "Plate some of this up for me while I change my clothes."

"Do you want some wine?"

"I had some earlier, but why not? Have you heard from Rachel?"

I was surprised he even brought her name up because he had already found a replacement. "Not a peep."

While he was changing, I made a plate for him — chicken, vegetables, and some store-bought macaroni and cheese. As the food warmed in the microwave, I opened the bottle of wine. I didn't know how long he would be upstairs, so I had to be quick. I took the packet of crushed up sleeping pills out of my back pocket and poured the white powder into a glass before adding a couple of drops of wine. The wine turned a muted shade of purple as I swished it around. I poured a fresh glass of wine and dumped the sleeping pill mixture in to top it off. I washed the old glass, dried it, and put it back in the cupboard. Footsteps. My pulse quickened. I took a deep breath. This was it.

We ate in silence at the dining room table, him on one end, me on the other. About six feet of oak between us that might as well have been wider than the ocean. I thought he'd want to talk about Rachel since he brought her name up earlier, but he kept his head down and finished his dinner in seven minutes flat.

"That was good chicken. Where did you get it?"

"Across town. Near Eden's house." Pause for reaction. Nothing. Stone-faced as usual. "If you like it, I can get it again."

"It's all right." He hadn't touched his wine but took it with him when he left the table. He sat in his recliner and turned on the television. Slowly, he sipped out of the glass. I stood in the kitchen, cleaning up, checking on him at every turn. Within a half an hour, he was knocked out, mouth open, snoring.

When I thought he was in a deep sleep, I carefully pried the glass from his fingers. I washed it to get rid of any residue left behind from the sleeping pill and put it back on the shelf with the others. With a pair of latex gloves, I took a new glass with fresh wine and pressed it up against his lips before placing it back in his hand.

Usually when he took a sleeping pill, he was out for the rest of the night. This was two or three sleeping pills plus wine, so for all I knew, I'd just killed him. Blood rushed in my ears like a violent ocean wave as my breathing became shallow. It was one thing to plan. It was another to act on it.

Eden got off work a little before ten that night.

I pulled my hair back in a ponytail, twisted it, and pinned it to my head. The front of my hair, I parted on the side and slicked it back with a bit of gel. I took my earrings out and all my makeup off.

When it was closer to nine o'clock, I grabbed the gym bag out of the back of my closet and changed into the pants and boots I had stashed in there. On the way out the door, I grabbed the keys to my father's car, an old jacket of his out of the coat closet, and a knife from the kitchen drawer. I popped the trunk and placed the bag next to the spare tire and the tire iron. Dad didn't bother putting them back properly after having the tire fixed.

When I got to the restaurant where Eden worked, I parked next to her car and waited. I kept my left arm up to shield my face, so no one could actually see me full on. But I made sure they saw me. I left the car running with the lights on.

Around quarter to ten, I heard Eden and a few others laughing as they came out the back door of the restaurant. As Eden was about to unlock her car, I lowered the passenger-side window.

"Hey," I said, keeping my voice soft and low, so no one would hear me. "Do you want to see the stars? It's a perfect night for it."

Without a word, she opened the door and got in. I hid my hands from the dome light, so she wouldn't see I was wearing latex gloves. They were practically invisible anyway, especially in the dark, but I didn't want her asking questions until I drove away.

"What are you doing with your father's car?"

"He's all depressed and shit and passed out in the chair, so I thought I'd take it for a spin. I never get to drive it, and I love this car. So, do you want to go for a drive?"

"Yeah, sure. Why are you dressed like that?"

I drove off before answering. "Like what?"

"In those raggedy old clothes. And why's your hair pulled up like that?"

"I was experimenting with a French twist. Does it look stupid?"

She didn't answer right away. "It could use a more refined touch. Do you want me to fix it for you?"

"No. Nobody's going to see it but you and me. How was work?"

"I made about $100 in tips. That's how good it was."

"Are you going to buy yourself something nice?"

"I'm saving up for my trip to Texas to visit my father at Christmas. That's what I've been wanting to talk to you about. Well, part of it." She started to say more but stopped before starting again. "I'm going to drop out of school and move to Texas. I'll get my GED down there, but…"

"What, why? I thought you were going to college."

"I will, but I have to take care of a few things first." Her hands cradled her baby bump. It sounded like she was going to run away and hide to keep the baby.

I changed the subject quickly. "I brought the telescope."

"Great. I haven't looked out of a telescope in years, since my father left, actually."

I turned on the dirt road that went up the hill to Point Lookout. Lucky for me, the sky was clear and full of stars, playing right into my lie. "Just look at all those things."

"I know. I never get to see them in town with all the lights."

"Makes you feel small, doesn't it?"

"Smaller, you mean." She giggled.

I was growing impatient, so I drove faster, not caring that the road was full of potholes and sharp turns. Eden gripped the door handle and kept one hand pressed against the dashboard but never asked me to slow down. Soon, I came to the perfect spot. It was kind of tucked away in the woods off from the main road and not really a good place to set up a telescope. Eden noticed this right away.

"Why did you stop here?"

"Could you help me get the telescope out the back? It's in the trunk."

She shrugged. "Okay, if you say so."

She got out the passenger side, and I met her around the back from the driver side. As soon as I lifted the trunk, I grabbed the tire iron and hit her over the

147

head. She fell to the ground. Every inch of me came alive, twitching with activity. I felt the greatest sense of relief I had ever known.

Sixteen

By the time I got home, it was past midnight. My father was still asleep in the chair. I tracked the muddy boots through the house, up the stairs, and right to his bedroom. As I undressed out of his clothes, I kept the blood-covered latex gloves on to leave some traces in his room. I stuffed the bloody clothes into the gym bag and shoved it deep in the back of his closet before I jumped into his shower, scrubbed clean, and put on fresh pajamas.

I changed the time on all the clocks in the house to 9:30 and woke my father. The pills certainly worked. He was practically comatose. Even after rocking his body back and forth, he didn't wake up until I shouted his name.

"Wha—?"

"It's time to go to bed. You fell asleep in the chair."

Disoriented, he rubbed his eyes. "What time is it?"

"It's almost ten o'clock. Do you want me to help you upstairs?"

He tried to stand but fell back into the chair. My father wasn't one to take help from anyone, but he seemed pretty out of it, so I offered again. Surprisingly, he leaned on me as I walked him upstairs. This was probably the closest I had ever been to this man, and it was the creepiest feeling I ever experienced. He flopped onto his bed, and I left him there splayed out, feet dangling off the side.

Once I knew he was asleep, I changed all the clocks in the house back to the right time. I had worked up an appetite, so I made myself a sandwich and ate it standing at the sink, something my father never let me do. The house was quiet, and, for once, I didn't feel scared.

The next morning, Dad came into my bedroom and woke me up. He sat on my bed, tapped on my shoulder like he was touching toxic waste, and looked at me solemnly. "You awake?"

"Obviously."

He swished what looked like a Bloody Mary around in a tall glass.

"Too much to drink last night?"

"Don't be a smartass." He took a swig from the glass, grimacing as he swallowed. "I have some bad news." I had never heard this voice before, never seen this side of him before.

"Did something happen to Rachel?"

"What? No." He squeezed his eyes shut and shook his head. "Eden's mother is downstairs and wants to talk to you. Your little friend never came home last night."

I shot upright. "What do you mean?"

"Just go downstairs and talk with her." He rubbed his forehead. "It's too early for this."

Her mother here already? I hadn't counted on her mother. In fact, I hadn't counted on looking into the woman's eyes ever again.

"Rachel was always better at handling these things, so don't screw it up. Don't say something stupid."

"Got it. Thanks." Even in a moment of life-altering news, my father still found a way to insult me. "Tell her I'll be down in a minute."

"Hurry it up. Don't leave me alone with her."

"She won't bite."

"You sure are bitchy this morning."

"Can I at least brush my teeth?"

"I'm timing you."

I raced to the bathroom and splashed cold water on my face. It didn't matter if Dad was timing me. He couldn't hurt me any more than he already has.

Mrs. Rhodes wasn't supposed to show up at my house, asking about Eden. That wasn't part of the plan. She was supposed to get a visit from the police after she had reported her daughter missing. The police were supposed to ask *her* the questions. She wasn't supposed to come here asking *me* the questions. This was escalating a lot faster than I had planned.

I practiced my poker face in the mirror so when Eden's mother talked with me, I wouldn't flinch. The image in the mirror was the same as the day before, but

I was different. It was so easy, easier than I ever thought it would be.

"Mrs. Rhodes, what's going on?"

She sat on the couch twisting a tissue around her finger. A woman who looked just like her sat beside her, comforting her.

"My father said you wanted to talk to me."

She jumped up and clutched my arms, digging her nails in my flesh. "Do you have any idea where Eden is?"

"The last time I saw her was on Friday at school. What happened?"

"She never came home last night. I'm usually in bed on the nights she works late. She never came home. Have you spoken to her?"

My father hovered about in the corner of the room, keeping his eyes fixated on the floor.

"Like I said, the last time I saw or spoke with her was on Friday at school. I haven't gotten any messages from her."

"What did she say to you on Friday? Did she tell you what she was going to be doing? Did she say anything about meeting up with a guy? I know she's been sneaking off with someone so don't lie for her."

I shot a quick glance over to my father in time to see the color drain from his face.

"Do you know anything about it?"

Why, yes, I do. And he's standing right over there.

152

She lunged at me again. "Come on, Christa, I'm desperate."

"She told me she had to work. That was it. We never do much of anything on the weekends anyway. I'm sure she's fine. She's probably with one of her other friends."

"She's not answering her phone."

That's because I crushed it with my boot and threw it in the woods.

"Can I get you something, Mrs. Rhodes?" my father said. "Maybe something a little on the strong side?"

She shook her head. "I'll stop by the restaurant to see if they know anything before I go to the police and report her missing."

"I'll try texting her. If I hear anything, I'll tell her to get home." I patted her on the back.

"Could you, please? This isn't like her. She's a good kid."

"I'll call our teammates. Maybe one of them knows something."

"Thanks, honey. I feel so badly for barging in on a Sunday morning."

"Don't," Dad and I said at the same time.

After Mrs. Rhodes left, Dad and I glowered at each other. He eased himself into his favorite chair, nodding his head. "Well, that's sobering."

"I'm sure she's fine. She's always doing stuff like this, to be honest."

"Maybe you should call your teammates like you said."

Calling my teammates wasn't part of the plan either, but since I said I was going to do it, I would. It would make me look less suspicious if I did it. Had to show concern for my missing friend.

My hands shook as I dug out the contact list for the team. I sat on the edge of the bed, biting my lip and bouncing my knee.

Janel was the first one I called. Her phone went straight to voicemail. "Hey. It's your favorite person. Eden's missing. If you might know where she is, give her mom a call." I tried Miko next. Then Leesa. It was early Sunday morning. No one was going to answer their phone, so I left the same message, minus the favorite person part, with all of them. My job was done.

By then, my stomach had a sour, burning sensation swirling around in it. I raced to the bathroom and took a couple of deep breaths. I needed to get a grip. I hopped in the shower and let the hot water calm me. The Zen moment didn't last long. Dad pounded on the door, jolting me back to reality.

"Be out in a minute."

"You should probably come downstairs and watch the news."

"I can't hear you through the door."

The door opened a crack. "You'll have to see it for yourself, but maybe it has something to do with your friend."

I shut the water off. "All right. Coming."

I took my time getting dressed, even braided my hair. When I got downstairs, I found Dad standing in front of the television with his mouth hanging open.

"What's going on?"

He pointed at the TV. A local reporter stood in front of a wooded area with police tape fluttering in the wind behind her.

"Someone found a fetus near the Point Lookout area."

"A what?"

"A fetus, an unborn baby. It's the most amazing thing. The guy's dog found it in the weeds and dropped it at his owner's feet."

"Dammit." I heard the words come out of my mouth but couldn't believe I reacted out loud. Dad had a massive hangover, so he might not have heard me.

"Did you say something?"

"I said, that's creepy."

"He said when the dog finally let go of it, he realized it was a fetus."

"You learned all of that while I was upstairs?"

"You've been up there over an hour. When I heard about your little friend, I turned on the news. Hang on, there's the reporter. Listen." He turned the volume up until it was blasting but after a groan and a cringe, he quickly turned it back down.

I sat on the edge of the sofa, listening to every detail the reporter had to say.

"As of right now, there's a lot of speculation as to what happened. We've heard premature birth from one source, botched abortion from another. If that's the case, the mother might be seeking medical attention in the area. All the local hospitals have been alerted. Police are encouraging anyone with information to come forward. The police found evidence at the scene suggesting another person might have been involved. There are two sets of footprints and a bloody shirt with initials embroidered on the pocket. They're not telling us what those initials are."

"Holy shit," Dad said under his breath.

That's right, Dad, you should be afraid. That was your baby. They're going to discover its DNA, and the trail will lead right back to you.

I hugged my knees to my chest. This was all happening too fast. I figured maybe a week or two before they found her or the baby, but since it was escalating quickly, I would have to act shocked like everyone else hearing this for the first time.

"Why do you think this has anything to do with Eden?" I asked.

"Missing girl. Fetus. Do the math."

"That's a big leap, don't you think?"

"Was she pregnant?"

Like you didn't know this. "She never said anything to me about it. Did she say anything to you?"

Dad jerked his head and squished up his face in a poor attempt at being offended and ran off to the kitchen. "Why would she say anything to me?"

156

"I don't know. She seemed to like you a lot." I rocked back and forth, resting my chin on my knees, pretending to be worried.

"You better eat some breakfast. This is probably going to be a long day."

"I can't think of eating right now." That was the truth. Even after that shower, I felt like a perfect storm of nerves.

Dad came out of the kitchen carrying a bowl of cereal. "Eat."

I took it, reluctantly. And that was when he finally noticed the mud on the carpet.

"What is this?" He followed the path of clumped dirt from the garage all the way up the stairs with his eyes. "Why is there mud in the house?"

Now was my chance to fuck with him. "I thought you knew."

"Why would I know?"

"You went out last night."

"I did?"

"Yeah, don't you remember?"

"No. When was this?" He turned to face me, hands on his hips, genuinely confused.

"About ten, I guess. I was half asleep when I heard you pull out of the garage. You don't remember?"

I could tell he was thinking about it.

"The last thing I remember was eating dinner."

"You don't remember anything about last night, anything at all?"

"Why don't you tell me since you seem to know everything."

"After dinner, you sat in your chair and turned on ESPN. I went upstairs to do my homework—"

"On a Saturday night?"

"I had a paper to write."

"All right, what else?"

"I must've fallen asleep around 9:30 or so. Around ten, I heard your car start and the garage door open and close, and that was that."

"What time did I get home, Christa?"

I was losing him. He was seeing through my game. "I have no idea. I was asleep until you woke me up this morning."

"Nonsense. I want this mud cleaned up by the time I come downstairs."

As soon as he was out of earshot, I snorted a giggle. The games have just begun, Daddy.

Seventeen

I had hoped all the kids at school would be talking about the baby found in the woods at Point Lookout. I was hoping they'd make the connection between the baby and Eden's sudden absence like my father had done. Nope. Not these idiots. Of course, they didn't know what I knew. I was the one with the secret. I had all the answers, but nobody came to me with any questions.

When I took a seat at my desk in homeroom, some of my classmates stole glances at me and whispered. Still, nobody mumbled her name to me. I was her best friend. Where was the sympathy? Maybe I didn't look sad enough. How was I supposed to be acting? Remorseful and wringing my hands? Hunched over with dark circles under my eyes from a long night of worry and no sleep? If I feigned remorse too soon, I'd look guilty. Others would see through the act and point fingers and whisper. If I didn't express enough emotion, same thing. But I wanted to talk about it, wanted to speak her name, wanted to know what they were thinking so badly. I slumped down in my seat and rested my chin on my chest, hoping to get their attention. Was that pathetic looking enough?

The homeroom teacher came in and took attendance. When she got to my name, she paused. Everyone in the room turned to me at the same time, like it was choreographed.

"Feeling okay, Ms. Pierce?" Mrs. Clark said.

I shot upright in my seat. "Yeah. Why?" Were my actions showing on my face already? Was I giving something away unintentionally?

"You look a little flushed."

I patted my cheeks with the palms of my hands. Some kids started laughing. "I don't feel hot."

"Okay, but you don't look well." Mrs. Clark finished taking attendance. I sat back and studied everyone's face as she called off their names.

In the hallway between classes, kids gawked at me, whispering, pointing as I passed by. I didn't hear what they said, but after third period, I had had enough. I ran off to the bathroom to splash cold water on my face. Mrs. Clark was right. I was flushed. My face wasn't a subtle shade of pink either. I hadn't had any tea or coffee that morning, yet I found myself with a case of the shakes. It was like that all morning long until my lunch period when everyone was distracted by food and hanging out.

When I sat down at the table with my fellow running buddies, I acted disinterested in their conversation, nibbling on the mac 'n' cheese.

"Where do you think she could be?" Janel said to the whole table. "I wonder if she ran off to Texas to be with her dad."

"Her mother already reported her missing to the police," Miko said. "I doubt she's in Texas. She would've said something to her mom, wouldn't she?"

"She was pregnant," Leesa said. "And seeing some old dude."

Miko made a gagging noise. "Disgusting."

"Some old dude?" I wanted to know, had to know, if they were talking about my father. "Where did you hear that?"

Leesa's face turned red. "Oops. I wasn't supposed to tell anyone."

Eden lied when I asked if she was pregnant yet she'd told someone like Leesa. "When did she tell you?"

"A couple months ago."

"A couple months ago?" All the heat pulled away from the surface of my skin. "Why didn't she tell me?"

No one said anything. They stole glances at each other and picked at their food.

"What's going on?"

"She wasn't sure who the father was," Leesa said, backpedaling.

"That is so not the point." My voice cut through the noise of the cafeteria. Everyone at the table surrounding ours turned, curious about the fuss. "I was her best friend, and she didn't tell me she was pregnant."

Janel threw her head back and laughed. "Best friend? She didn't even like you."

161

"Janel," Miko said, smacking her with the back of her hand. "Why would you say something like that?"

This might have been a jab at me because she knew how much I liked Eden or at least pretended to like her. "Yeah, why would you say something like that?" I glared at her, but Janel wasn't intimidated by me in the least. She could kick my ass in a fight.

"Because it's true. Christa, you're deluded. If you think Eden is your best friend, fine, but that doesn't make it true. I'm not going to sugarcoat it, okay. She only hung out with you because you had money. Do you know how many times she'd call me after you left her house and made fun of you? Do you know what she said after the first time she went to your house? Something to do with the shoes."

Miko and Leesa kept their eyes on their lunch trays and shook their heads slowly.

"I can't believe you're doing this," Miko said, under her breath. "Especially right now."

"She's going to hear it sooner or later," Janel said, defiantly.

"What did she say about me?"

I was beginning to look like an idiot. I used Eden to get at my father. It backfired because he ended up liking her. A little too much. The two of them fucking wasn't part of the plan. Her getting pregnant was a complication that was dealt with.

Leesa slammed her hand on the table. "You guys, stop it. Eden is missing. That might've been her baby in the woods, and you guys are fighting about stupid shit."

162

"Leesa's right," Miko said. "I don't want to be a part of this." She stabbed her mac 'n' cheese with her fork. "And now my food is cold."

My face burned with anger. "No, I want to know what she said. Did you know she was pregnant, Janel?"

"Anyone with eyes could tell she was pregnant, Christa. Didn't you see her bump? You know, for someone so smart, you're pretty dumb."

"Yes, I saw her bump, but I didn't think it was my business to ask." That was what I said because I didn't want anyone knowing Eden lied to my face when I did ask. The lie only confirmed my suspicion that my father got her pregnant. If she didn't have anything to hide, she would have confided in me.

"A best friend would have asked."

Miko and Leesa picked up their trays and left the table, leaving me alone with Janel and her bitchiness.

"Now that they're gone, you can tell me everything."

"They're right. Eden is missing. We shouldn't be fighting. I know you don't think I like you, but the reason I'm telling you this is because I do like you. It bothered me that she talked shit about you behind your back and kissed your ass when you guys were together. At least I have the guts to say it to your face. Eden isn't as innocent as you think. She's a compulsive liar. Don't get me wrong, I really like her, but I don't trust her. I'm surprised you didn't see it."

"Are you saying our whole friendship was a lie? Why would she do that?"

"Maybe because she was poor and wanted to see how the other half lived. Maybe she thought you could give her something, like that bracelet."

My heart skipped a beat. *Oh boy, here we go. Play it off, Christa. Find out what she knows.* "What bracelet?"

"That bracelet you bought her. The one with the roses. She went on and on about it." Janel shook her head in disbelief. "Seriously? She lied about that, too?"

"I don't know anything about a bracelet."

Janel laughed. "Amazing. Now I'm wondering how much she played me. Sorry for telling you all this, but maybe it's good you know. Maybe I should've told you sooner."

"Maybe you should have."

"Who knows, Christa, maybe she was like that with everyone, not just you. Who knows what she said about me behind my back. It's time for class. You better shove that food in your face hole before it's too late. I'll see you later, k?"

"Yeah, later."

I didn't bother finishing my lunch. I wanted to throw it across the room. Instead, I threw everything, including the tray, in the trash and headed for my next class.

As I turned the corner to go upstairs, I found a group of kids huddled together, cupping their mouths, eyes wide open. Within seconds someone had screamed *Oh my God.* The small crowd broke open. Miko was in tears, shaking, clutching her phone to her chest. Janel and Leesa wrapped their arms around her.

164

I rushed over to them. "What's going on?"

"Miko just checked the news on her phone." Janel struggled to speak, her chin trembling, her eyes filling with tears. "The police found Eden's body. They think she's been…" She squeezed her eyes shut. Tears raced down her cheeks. "They say she was murdered. The monster cut the baby out of her stomach."

I was hardly a monster. The blood rushed from my head down to my feet. Everything turned black. I stumbled backwards into the display case for the Forensics' team. The jolt brought me back quickly. The reaction might have been for a different reason than that of my classmates, but it was convincing enough. I saw how the other kids were reacting and did the same or they would think I really was a monster. I let out a yelp and dropped to the floor, burying my face in my hands, trying to work up a few tears.

The rest of the day was a blur. I tried checking the internet from my phone to read the latest news, but a teacher caught me every time. They all told me not to obsess and look at the news because it would only make me sick. I wasn't worried about being sick. I was wondering how the investigation was going, if they'd found any evidence that could point to me when I'd tried my best to have it all point back to my father.

As soon as I got home, I dropped my bag at the door and ran to the television, hoping the news would be playing non-stop coverage of Eden's death.

It took some time, but I found a breaking news segment on one of the local channels. Someone was talking about it. Mostly, it was about how her mother identified the body and hinted at the evidence they found at the scene. The crime scene investigators had worked fast. My mind was so focused on the television, I forgot to breathe.

"I just received word from authorities that a few witnesses have come forward and have given a description of the car that picked the victim up on the night of the murder." It was the same newscaster who broke the news when they found the baby's body in the woods of Point Lookout.

My mouth went dry waiting for her to finish.

"On the night of Eden's disappearance, someone driving an older model Mercedes-Benz was parked in the parking lot after the restaurant had already closed. The man spoke to Eden briefly before she got in the car. Eyewitnesses said there was no argument or struggle and that Eden appeared to know the person. No one could identify the driver of the vehicle, but they all believe the driver to be a white male. One of the victim's co-workers, who is an old car enthusiast, gave a detailed description of the car. The police are now running a search on that particular make and model."

I leaned back, digging my nails in the leather of the arm of the chair.

"Princess? What are you doing? Why aren't you doing your homework?"

I jumped up, nearly stumbling over my own feet. "Geez, Dad. You scared the crap out of me."

"Obviously. But what are your shoes doing on, and why is your stuff laying on the floor by the door?"

I pointed to the television. "They found Eden."

"Oh." He took a sharp breath. "Is she alive?"

"The police found her body this morning."

My father glared at me, his eyes intense and questioning. Even after all of this, I was still intimidated by something as simple as a look. "For someone who just lost her friend, you're handling it rather well."

"I'm in shock. I mean, I just turned on the news and heard. I'm still processing it."

"I would imagine so. If you need something to calm your nerves, I give you permission to have a small glass of wine."

"No, thanks." I didn't want to be numb. I needed clarity.

I stayed glued to the television for the rest of the evening. Completely out of character, Dad ordered takeout Chinese and tried to get me to eat, but I was too anxious. So far, nobody came forward to identify me as the person driving the car. So far, it was only a male driving a Mercedes. My father's Mercedes. Dad didn't stick around to watch the news to hear them talking about his car. I hoped they'd talk about the car on the news again while he was in the room so I could see his reaction.

After Jeopardy, another breaking news bulletin came on. My father was in the room with me this time, and he wasn't getting up to leave.

"Police are releasing the surveillance video of the night Eden Rhodes went missing," the reporter said. "Unfortunately, the quality of the video is blurry, but you can see her getting in the car and driving away."

We both leaned closer to the TV as the video played. It was over within seconds. Out of the corner of my eye, I caught my father staring intently at the screen, his eyebrows knitted together.

"Can you see what kind of car it is?" I asked, hoping my father would recognize his car immediately.

He lifted a glass of scotch to his lips.

It looked like he wasn't catching on, so I tried again. "They said it was a Mercedes-Benz."

He choked on his drink. "When did they say that?"

"Right before you came home. A red Mercedes. Hey, wait a minute. You drive a red Mercedes, don't you, Daddy?"

He placed his drink on a coaster calmly and went upstairs.

I sat and smiled. Everything was going better than I expected. A little faster than I had hoped, but things were falling into place. Soon they'll discover the evidence and it will all lead back to him.

My father had blacked out that night. He couldn't remember a thing, and I was doing my best to fill in the blanks with a bunch of lies. Unless he suddenly remembered everything, I was set. As far as I was concerned, I was asleep by 9:30. Tired after a long day. Since I couldn't vouch for his whereabouts, he didn't have an alibi.

The phone my mother and I used to communicate with each other rang, startling me. When I'd rushed home to turn on the news, I'd dropped my bag by the door, forgetting to turn the phone off. I had to hurry and answer it before my father heard it ringing. It stopped before I got to it. Mom had left a voicemail message. I hid in the laundry room to listen to it. *"Just found out about your friend. Are you all right? Call me when you can."*

Before texting back, I cracked the door open to see if my father was nearby, spying on me.

Me: Can't talk now. Still in shock. Where are you?

Mom: In Ohio, cleaning out a room in my sister's house. There's another bedroom waiting for you.

Me: Can't wait to sleep in it. It won't be long now. Will call soon.

News about Eden's death was spreading way too fast. It was one thing for it to spread in this town, but all the way in Ohio? How had she heard. From her friend in the coffee shop, maybe? No matter what happened next, I had to be careful. The next few days were going to be tricky. I planted just the right amount of evidence so the trail led right back to my father. All I had to do was keep quiet and watch him unravel.

Eighteen

Dad snatched the car keys from my hand. "Get in the car."

"Why?"

"Princess, there's a murderer on the loose, and you knew the victim. I'm not about to let something happen to you."

He would love for me to believe this was a show of affection, but I knew better. He wasn't concerned for me; he was worried someone would see his car.

"You either take the bus or let me drive you to school. And I'm pretty sure you don't want to ride the bus. Was it you who complained some of the kids teased her all the time, or was that someone else? Do you remember how miserable you were?"

"But why are we taking *my* car?"

"Mine is leaking oil."

I bit my lip to hide my smile. "How long is this going to last?"

"Until they catch the killer. Now, get in the car or I'm going to be late for work. If I'm late, you're not going to like it."

Faking reluctance, I let him drive me to school. It felt like old times. Before he bought me a car for my sixteenth birthday, we must have driven past the road that led to Point Lookout a million times. My natural inclination was to stare out the window and zone out to deal with the usual tension in the car. This time I was looking toward Point Lookout. I wanted to know what was going on at the crime scene. I wanted to know what they were saying about the evidence they found. Did they find the bracelet? Would they put two and two together when they saw the initials MJP on the shirt and start knocking on my father's door?

"Look away, Princess." My father's booming voice filled the small car.

"Christa."

"You'll always be Princess to me."

It was hard to know what my father was feeling about all this considering he had sex with Eden and that was his baby they discovered in the woods. If it was bothering him, if he was worried, he sure didn't act like it, but Dad was so good at masking his emotions when it was needed. I, on the other hand, had to pretend to be sad before everyone started wondering why I wasn't more upset.

I rested my head against the window, letting out long sighs. In the side mirror, I saw a state police car behind us. My body stiffened. The car was tailgating us. I kept waiting for the lights to go on as we drove along, but nothing happened. Dad took the exit to my school. The cop drove off the same exit and followed us the rest of the way. My heart never beat so hard before, even after a race. I tried to steady my breathing, but my body wasn't cooperating.

It was madness at school. Cop cars and lights everywhere. All the school administrators were standing on the sidewalk directing students as they filed off the buses. Teachers chased kids into the building before they had a chance to huddle together like they normally did before class started. A few police officers were directing cars into the student parking lot.

"Pandemonium," Dad said, softly. "Do you want me to take you home?"

I was tempted to say yes. But how would it look if I skipped school? "Aren't you worried about being late?"

He checked his watch. "I do have a meeting first thing. Out. Don't talk to the police unless our lawyer is present. I'll give him a call as soon as I get to work."

"Nothing would embarrass me more."

"It's what I pay him for. You tell them that you refuse to talk to the authorities until your lawyer arrives."

Only guilty people needed lawyers. Did he think I was guilty? "Why would I need a lawyer?"

"You're not an adult yet, and the police can't talk to you unless you have someone with you. Do you want me to go in there with you? I'm sure you'd love that. Now, get to class, Princess."

I climbed out of the car and slammed the door. "My name is Christa."

My knees grew weak as I watched a sea of blue uniforms hovering around the principal's office. The radios clipped to their shoulders buzzed with snippets of official sounding coded words. Their chests were puffed out from the body armor under their shirts. If the administration wanted to alarm the students, this would be the way to do it. Even if they weren't watching me specifically, I was convinced they were and could see right through my efforts to act normal. Walking the hall suddenly felt like walking on slippery rocks in a creek bed. My arm swing felt out of sync with the rest of me, making me hyper-aware of the movement. I stared at the floor as I walked past them to get to home room, but the teachers redirected us to the auditorium.

"What's going on?" I asked Ms. Martinez.

"You'll see," she said, curtly.

None of the teachers looked to be in the mood to talk, so I didn't press for more details.

When I entered the auditorium, I felt everyone's eyes on me, like I was naked. Miko and Leesa ran over and hugged me. Even Janel joined in.

"I can't believe this," Leesa said. "I feel so bad for everything I said about her yesterday."

"You didn't know," Miko said, wiping her face with the sleeve of her shirt.

"I'm in shock," was all I could say. Shock was a good explanation for my lack of emotion, and they accepted it. "It seems so surreal, like a bad dream that I can't wake up from."

"I know," Janel said. "I couldn't sleep last night. Thinking about what happened to her made me sick to my stomach."

"I slept with the lights on," Miko said. "Good thing I have a dog to keep me company."

My legs were itchy and restless. The doorway to the auditorium was a bottleneck of students and teachers. Never had I wanted to push my way out of a place more than at that time. "Why are we meeting in here, do you know?" I asked.

"I'm sure it has something to do with Eden," Leesa said, her lip quivering.

Since I couldn't escape this, it was probably a good idea if I worked up some kind of response to everything that was happening around me. I watched Leesa closely. She was always the emotional one in our group. Her eyes were bloodshot from crying. I couldn't fake that. It looked like she had slept in her clothes and hadn't brushed her hair. It was too late for that since I made some effort this morning. But she seemed distant, distracted, her face an obvious expression of grief. She stared at the floor a lot, wiped her face with the sleeve of her baggy sweater, bit her lip, and when she spoke to anyone, she answered softly, clipping her sentences and trailing off at the end. Those actions I could manage, except for using my sleeve as a tissue. Dad would whack me a good one if I ever did that, but he wasn't here, and I had to put on a show.

"Everyone, take your seats," the principal said. He stood on stage holding a microphone in one hand and

174

waving the other one in the air to get everyone's attention. The school nurse, several teachers, and a few official looking people stood behind him.

Real emotions were now starting to settle in, but they weren't the ones my friends were experiencing, the ones I needed to show. Ever since I'd planned to get rid of Eden, I never imagined I'd get caught. I never planned this far out.

The others must know what I had done. The pressure showed on my face, I was sure of it. Sooner or later, I would crack. Dad always knew when I lied. Others would certainly see it, too. What made me think I could get away with this?

"Everyone. Pay attention, please. We have a lot to cover this morning." The principal stood, waiting for the noise to die down. "As you may have heard by now…" His voice cracked. He cleared his throat a few times while his chin quivered. "We lost one of our own recently. She was a bright, lively girl, a top student and athlete. A lot of you might be feeling confused and scared. We have counselors on hand if you need to speak with someone. After this assembly, if you wish to make an appointment, please line up outside the main office. We also have a couple of detectives on hand who would like to address you. Detective Gonzales." He handed the microphone to a man dressed in a suit and tie. I always thought cops dressed in uniforms.

"Good morning. My name is Detective Gonzales, and this is my partner, Detective Naylor." A short woman dressed in an over-sized coat stepped forward and nodded her head before stepping back. "We'll keep this short so you can have time to process this tragedy. This investigation is ongoing. We'll want to talk with some of you, especially if you were close to the victim. If you know anything and want to remain anonymous, there's a tip line you can call. Administration has hung posters in the hallways and in your classrooms with the numbers in case you need to reach us. Some of you may want to have a parent present when we speak with you. Some of you may need to come to the station. Don't panic. This is standard operating procedure. You aren't in any trouble. We only want to find who did this to your classmate. That's all I have. All right, Principal Martin, back to you."

As the principal discussed how things were going to go down, I went over my story in my head, working up a few tears. I covered my face and shook my body like I was sobbing, copying Rachel the night she found out about Eden and Dad, imitating Leesa who had turned into a slobbering mess. Within a few seconds my brain responded to the physical act, and I produced actual tears. It was the weirdest thing.

Leesa rested her head on my shoulder and cried. "How could anyone hurt her?"

"I don't know," I said, sniffling like her.

Leesa sat up and stared at me with those puffy, bloodshot eyes of hers. "I wish I could be as calm as you." She shook her head. "How do you do it?"

What? I thought for sure my show was more obvious. I'd have to try harder at looking pathetic. I quivered my chin, squished up my eyes, and pushed out a few high-pitched whimpers before burying my face in my hands.

"I'm sorry," Leesa said, holding me. "I guess everyone copes in different ways."

Soon everyone around me gathered in a huddle and hugged and cried and asked questions that no one could answer. But me.

"Christa Pierce?" Principal Martin said as I stepped into the hallway and headed toward the front doors. "Could you come to my office, please?" He was flanked by the two detectives, both of them with concerned, sympathetic eyes. "We'd like to talk to you for a bit. I heard you were close with Eden, and we're hoping you might shed some light on a few things."

I gulped. Even with all the noise in the hallway, everyone around me heard it.

"No worries, this isn't that kind of questioning," Detective Gonzales said. His voice was strong and confident, making me feel even more nervous. "We're just trying to put the pieces together."

"The guidance counselor and I will be in the room with you," Principal Martin said, reassuringly.

"Okay," was all I could say. Not like I could get out of it. Principal Martin was six-feet-five with two detectives by his side. All three of them were intimidating, and even if I was used to being intimidated by my father, this was different. I could take that nervousness and twist it into the emotions of losing my best friend, but I still had to check myself. Despite what they said, the two detectives would scrutinize everything I did, every move I made even if this wasn't an interrogation. That was their job. My legs twitched, wanting to sprint right out the doors, the feeling stronger than it was that morning as we gathered for the assembly.

"Right this way." Principal Martin opened the door for me where I found Rachel with open arms and a forced smile.

She tried to hug me, but I pushed her away. She stepped back, embarrassed. Her eyes were puffy and red from crying. "I've missed you."

"What are you doing here?"

"Don't be rude," she whispered. "Your dad called me."

"Who's this?" the principal asked.

"My stepmother."

"My husband, Dr. Michael Pierce,` asked me to be here."

"It isn't necessary," Detective Naylor said. "But since you're here."

While Rachel helped me get comfortable in the chair, I eyed the detectives as they took out notepads and pens.

"Now, I'll be asking you a few questions first," Principal Martin said. "If the detectives have any more questions for you, they'll probably want to see you down at the police station. This is nothing more than to find out what you know and if you need any counseling. I understand you two were close. Can I get you anything before we start? Some water?"

My mouth felt like it was full of cotton balls, so I agreed to the water. The guidance counselor filled a cone-shaped cup from the water cooler. The bubble and gurgle filled the quiet office. When I took hold of it, ripples formed in the cup. I had no idea I was shaking that badly. Rachel noticed and took the cup from me. She rubbed the small of my back gently.

"We can do this another time if you're not ready," Principal Martin said. "Would tomorrow be better?"

He must have seen the shaking. I didn't count on it being this hard. "No, I'm okay. I want you to find the monster who did this to her."

"Okay. First question: what was your relationship with Eden?"

"She was my best friend." That was the answer I gave, and I was going to use it to the very end.

"When was the last time you saw her?"

"The last time I saw and spoke with her was on Friday at school. I was hoping we could get together to hang out over the weekend, but she said she had to work."

"Did you know she was pregnant?"

"She never told me." I thought about mentioning that the other girls on our team knew, but decided against it. It wasn't time to bring them into it yet.

"Can I jump in here?" Detective Gonzales said.

"Let me finish first then if she's up to it you can ask her some questions."

"You're right. Carry on."

"Do you know if she was seeing anyone here at the school?"

Now was a good time to start leading them astray. "She was dating some guy from the other high school for a while. His name is Kyle Jenkins. I heard from one of the other girls yesterday that she was messing around with an older man."

The detectives perked up at my comment. Rachel dug her nails into my back.

"I don't know if that's true. It's probably gossip. She would've told me about it, I'm sure."

"I would assume so. One last question. Is there anything, no matter how insignificant it might seem, you could tell us? Anything like phone calls, comments that seem out of the ordinary, or anything. It may seem like nothing to you, but it might make a world of difference in finding the person who did this."

"I can't think of anything right now. It's so shocking. I can't stop watching the news."

"You should step away from the television," Detective Gonzales said. "It's unhealthy to obsess, especially when it's someone you were close to."

"I agree," Principal Martin said. "Take care of yourself first and surround yourself with people who care about you."

Not in my house.

"That brings me to my next question. Do you need someone to talk to? We have the resources if you do. We're going to be offering counseling over the next couple of weeks, so don't hesitate to come in and speak with someone if you need to. All right?"

"I might do that later. Right now, it's still sinking in."

"Okay, if there's nothing else, you can go. Since your stepmother is here, she can take you home unless you drove yourself. We'll resume classes tomorrow, but if you need some time off, we can make allowances. Since you're a senior and at the head of your class, it shouldn't be a problem at all."

Rachel and I stood to leave, but Detective Gonzales raised his hand in the air, stopping us. "Before you go. Christa, I'd like for you to stop at the station whenever you have some time. We'd like to ask you a few more questions. In-depth."

My throat tightened. "Of course."

"Since you were her best friend, I mean. Best friends know a lot of things, secrets and such or maybe something you overlooked. Plus, there's a piece of evidence we'd like you to look at. We want justice for this girl."

"We'll make arrangements," Rachel said. "If there's nothing else, I'd like to get her home. She doesn't look well."

When we got to the car, Rachel looked at me with daggers in her eyes. "What do you think you're doing?"

"What do you mean?"

"Why would you say anything about her having an affair with an older man? Are you trying to ruin your father?"

"Rachel, my father had sex with my best friend. She was pregnant with his baby, and now she's dead. Don't you think that looks suspicious?" I waited for a reaction, but nothing came. "Besides, I thought you left him. What are you even doing here?"

"News flash, Christa. Your father can't have kids."

Time stopped. My heart stopped. My breathing stopped. Everything stopped. "What do you mean he can't have kids? He had me, didn't he?"

"Your father had a vasectomy after you were born."

I tried to catch my breath. She was probably saying this to protect him, like she always did.

"Are you all right? If you're going to throw up, open the door. I just had the car detailed."

My head spun so fast, I thought I was going to barf. I wanted to burst the door open and run as far away as possible. "Let's just get going."

Rachel drove away from the school. The shadow of it played across the windshield.

"After I heard about what happened to Eden, I called your father. He said you might need me and asked me to come back."

This wasn't supposed to happen. "Are you moving back into the house?"

"I already spoke with a lawyer."

"That doesn't answer my question."

"No. He wanted me to move back in, but I won't. I'm only here for you."

"And to make sure his reputation doesn't get ruined. I don't understand you. After all he's put you through, you still defend him. He doesn't deserve your sympathy."

"You're right, but if it comes out he was having an affair with her, let it come out organically. There's no reason why you need to blurt it out like that."

But I had to get the ball rolling. They would find out eventually, but why not push things along more quickly? I wanted to get on with my life without him in it.

"Are you hungry?"

"No. Dad's been forcing me to eat. For once, I would like to eat when my body is ready."

She grew quiet for a minute. "How is he?"

I wasn't going to lie, and I wasn't going to hold back. Rachel was gone, and I liked it that way. Her being here could be trouble for me. She was dumb enough that she might provide an alibi for that bastard. "He's already moved on. I don't know who she is, but she's young and likes stupid movies, apparently." I watched Rachel out of the corner of my eye. She pursed her lips and tilted her head in recognition of what I had said. "You seriously didn't think he would sit around pining for you, did you?"

"I would've thought with the way he treated you through your life, you would turn out to be a better human being than you are, but I can see you are as cruel as he is."

"He made me that way."

"No, he didn't. You can only use him as a scapegoat for so long. I tried my best to be nice to you and to give you what little love you would let me give. You always kept me at a distance like your father. I should've left a long time ago when I still had the money. Oh well, I'm gone now. Look, I'm going to drop you off at the house. You can tell your father you're on your own. I refuse to help when it's not wanted, when I'm not wanted. The two of you are perfect for each other. I wish I had seen it sooner. Both of you disgust me."

I smiled. "If you had shown this much backbone from the beginning, I probably would've had more respect for you."

"You really are a bitch. Get out of my car."

I slammed the door. Rachel zipped away and disappeared. "Stupid, bitch."

I had bigger things to worry about than hurting Rachel's precious feelings. Without the baby's DNA pointing back to my dad, he didn't have a motive for killing his young, pregnant fling. The police weren't going to pin it on him without that major piece of evidence. The bracelet and shirt I planted weren't going to be enough to nail him. Dressing up to look like him, using his clothes, stealing his car—all a waste of time without the paternity.

Nineteen

As soon as Dad came home from work, I told him what had happened between Rachel and me before she had a chance to fill his head with a bunch of lies. As angry as she was, she'd exaggerate everything to make me look bad. He didn't seem to care. In fact, he seemed relieved she wasn't going to be hanging around. I thought I heard him mumble something about her bringing him down and getting in his way. In the way of his new girlfriend, probably.

"That would explain why she hasn't answered my calls," he said, casually as he fixed himself a drink. But when I told him the detective asked me to go to the police station to answer a few questions, he cared. "Did they say why? I don't understand. You hung out with each other, but you were hardly close."

"We were best friends."

"If you say so." He laughed the same way Janel had laughed when I told her Eden was my best friend. Everyone was making me look like a fool.

"Tell me everything the detectives said. What did the principal say?"

His questions came at me so fast, I felt myself shrinking. "I told you everything already."

"I'll call my lawyer."

"But..."

"But what?"

"They said I don't need an adult present."

"Nonsense. You're only seventeen."

"But..."

"But what, Christa? If you've got something on your mind, say it."

I hesitated.

"That's what I figured." He reached for his phone. "Keep quiet while I talk with the lawyer."

"I'm not a minor."

"Yes, you are. Besides, you're dumb enough to say the wrong thing to the cops. You can't trust those bastards. They have a way of twisting your words. While you're up..." He swished the ice cubes around in his glass.

I took a sniff of the leftover liquid. "What is this?"

"Scotch. Fresh ice. You know what, just bring the bottle."

While my father mumbled into the phone, I kept my ears trained to what he was saying. It wasn't much. "How about nine?" It looked like I was going to the station at nine. "I don't want her thinking she can get out of going to school. Can you drive her there?" And I was going to school afterward. "Did you get all that, Christa? I'll drop you off at the station at nine. The

186

lawyer will meet you there and drive you to school after."

It was useless to argue; I wasn't going to win. I gave Dad his fresh drink, the bottle of scotch, and cracked open a book.

Instead of going to my room to study, I curled up on the couch, waiting for the alcohol to turn him stupid. He was an embarrassingly sloppy drunk. I found him face down on the kitchen floor once after I heard a commotion in the middle of the night. He had opened a can of tomato soup and must have fallen before he even emptied the can into the pot. Thick red paste covered the walls, the floor, him. I went back to bed and left the mess for Rachel to clean up in the morning. He's done worse, like almost driving his car all the way through the garage.

With every tick-tock of that damn ugly kitchen clock, his eyes grew droopier, his shoulders hunched, and he could barely keep his head up.

"Is anything wrong, Dad?"

"Nothing is ever wrong, Christa."

"Are you sure? You look nervous about something."

He jerked his head in my direction, his eyes glassy. "What would I have to be nervous about?"

"I don't know. Maybe you're upset about Eden and the baby."

"What?"

"The baby. You forgot about the baby already?"

187

He blinked in slow motion. "Of course not." He tried to get out of the chair but fell backwards, spilling the drink in his lap. "Dammit."

"Poor little baby."

"Who?"

"Exactly."

His head fell to the side. It looked like I was losing him to the scotch.

"Aren't you afraid they'll find out about Eden?"

"Nope." With half-closed eyes, he smiled.

"Someone was asking about it."

"Impossible."

"Maybe she told somebody."

His eyes narrowed. "She promised she wouldn't."

"It's all over school."

His head bobbled around. "Little liar."

"Me or Eden?"

"Both of you."

"You can't keep secrets around this town for long."

He stared at me for a few beats. "Don't you have homework to do?"

Feeling victorious, I left him in his chair. Lawyer or no lawyer, I had to go to the police station and start pointing the finger at him.

The next morning, my father was still asleep in the chair when I walked out the door. I laughed as I started my car and revved the engine. He'd have to drive his own car to work, if he even had the balls to do it, and he'd go ballistic later that I didn't wake him to take me to the police station. His raging hangover would make things worse, but I didn't care.

The lawyer waited outside the police station, pacing the sidewalk. He seemed shocked to see only me.

"Where's your father?"

His name was Nathan Collins and could fit in my family. He was tall and blond with freckles dancing across the bridge of his nose, just like my father and me. And he was crooked, just like my father.

"Dad wasn't feeling up to coming." I wanted to ask if it would make me look suspicious by going in with a lawyer but realized that was a question a suspicious person would ask. How was I going to drop all these hints to frame my father with him in the room with me? "Can we do this fast so I can go to school?"

"Just answer the questions, carefully, and if I feel they're getting into an inappropriate area, I'll stop you. Remember, I can stop this conversation any time during the meeting. Okay?"

I nodded and took a deep breath. This was it. It was either the end of my father, or me.

The interrogation room was no bigger than my walk-in closet at home. It was a cold, gray room with an equally cold chair and table. The fluorescent lights above my head hummed and snapped.

Detective Naylor took a seat next to Detective Gonzales and studied me. She was clearly pregnant—something I didn't notice when I first met her in the

189

principal's office. I bet she had lots of thoughts and feelings about this case.

"Now, let's get this started, shall we?" Detective Gonzales said, opening a folder. He pulled out a stack of papers and a small baggie that held the bracelet that I had put on Eden's wrist before I rolled her body down the hill. "So, Christa, you were friends with Eden Rhodes, correct?"

I nodded.

Detective Gonzales put his hand to his ear. "I'm sorry?"

"Yes, I was best friends with Eden."

"And yet you didn't know she was pregnant. Is that correct?"

"She never told me she was pregnant."

"But did you know?"

"Isn't that the same thing?"

"Let's move on," the lawyer interrupted.

"Why are you here?" Detective Naylor said, leaning forward.

"Her father hired me."

"This isn't an interrogation."

I shot Mr. Collins a look. "It wasn't my choice, so can we get this over with? I have to get to school."

Detective Gonzales watched both of us for a beat before turning his attention to me. "Did she tell you or did you know she was seeing an older man?"

"No, she never said anything about it. I heard it from one of our teammates the other day."

"Was that the first time you heard of it?"

I hesitated, glanced away, looked back at him, and nodded. "Yes," I said, remembering he wanted me to speak my answers and not mime them.

He flipped through his notes. "You told Principal Martin that the last time you spoke and saw her was on Friday the day before she died. Is that correct?"

"Yes."

"What were you doing on Saturday night?"

"I thought you weren't interrogating her?" the lawyer said.

"That's all right," I said, touching his arm. "I have nothing to hide." My mouth went dry because it felt very much like I was being interrogated. Somehow, I had to ease into letting all of this information out without making it sound like I was trying to pin everything on my father. "I was at home that night. My father had gone out to the movies earlier with…a friend. I don't know who. When he came home, I had dinner waiting for him. I finished up my homework and ended up falling asleep at 9:30. I know it sounds pathetic, but I'm not much of a social creature. That's why I'll end up being valedictorian of my graduating class."

"Your father will verify this?"

I made attempts to speak. "Well, yes?"

"You don't sound certain. Why is that?"

I looked back and forth between the two detectives. "No, I'm certain. I was at home. My father…should be able to verify that."

"Was your father home that night?"

"Uh, yes."

"Was he or wasn't he?"

"I was asleep, so I wouldn't know."

Detective Gonzales scribbled something in his notebook. He reached for the baggie inside the envelope and held it up in front of my face. "Do you know what this is?"

"It looks like a bracelet."

"Have you ever seen it before?"

I placed my hands on top of the table and started picking at the polish on my fingernails. Nervous excitement coursed through my body. This could be effective in convincing them I was hiding something about my father. "Should I?"

"Have you seen it before, yes or no?"

A long, dramatic pause. "I might have."

Detective Gonzales' brown eyes bore a hole through me. "Look again to refresh your memory."

"Are you implying something?" the lawyer asked.

"I'm not implying anything. I only want a clear answer, and I *might have* isn't a clear answer."

I was blowing it. I started trembling and worked up a couple of tears.

"Are you okay, Christa?" Mr. Collins asked. "We can stop right now if you don't feel up to it."

"So, I'm right? You have seen this before, haven't you?"

I pinched the bridge of my nose. "Is "For My Princess" engraved on it?"

With my hand partially covering my eyes, I watched both detectives perk up.

"Yes, it is. Do you know where this came from?"

I took a deep breath. This was it. This was the moment I was going to destroy my father's life. "My dad gave it to me for my birthday."

"All right, that's enough." Mr. Collins wrapped his hand around my upper arm in a vice grip and pulled me to my feet. We were leaving, apparently. "That bracelet could've come from anybody."

"Sit down," Detective Gonzales said.

"She's not under arrest," Detective Naylor said. "She's not even under suspicion."

"Let her answer the questions."

I pulled my arm away. Hearing those words come out of Naylor's mouth gave me a boost of confidence. "I want to answer the questions."

"One more step over the line and this conversation is through." He stared sternly at the detectives. "Do you understand?"

"Sure." Detective Gonzales collected the scattered papers and placed them neatly back in the folder. "Now, Christa, tell me what you know about the bracelet."

"At my birthday dinner, my father gave me a box and inside was a bracelet with the words "For My Princess" inscribed on the back. My father always calls me Princess. I'm seventeen, and I hate it."

"I hear that," Detective Naylor said, laughing. "My father called me Princess my whole life, and I hated it. Until he died. Now I miss it." Maybe she was playing the good cop or whatever, but I wasn't falling for it.

"My father was talking with someone when he overheard me telling my stepmother I hated being called Princess, and when he sat down, he took the bracelet away from me. That was the last time I saw it. I don't know what happened to it after that."

"All right, we're through," the lawyer said, infuriated. He went to grab my arm again, but I broke away.

"I want to answer the questions, so we can find out who killed my friend."

"Maybe the girl stole the bracelet," the lawyer said. "We all know what kind of person she was."

"Hey!" Detective Naylor shot up out of her seat. "Watch it. The girl has a name. Eden Rhodes was a victim of a crime. Don't pull that courtroom drama in here."

"All right, all right," Detective Gonzales said, holding his hands up. "Let's calm down. You can go to school. We'll talk again soon."

I didn't want to go. I was on a roll. I didn't want to do this another time. The more interactions I had with the law, the worse it was for me because sooner or later, I'd slip up.

"Grab your things." The lawyer dragged me outside and spun me around. "What are you doing?"

He reminded me of my father when he got mad. "I'm answering the questions."

"Do you realize what you said makes it sound like your father had something to do with this? Why would you do that?"

"The detective asked a question, and I answered it. Can I go to school now?"

Nathan Collins threw his hands in the air and walked away.

After school, as I pulled in the garage, I saw that my father was still at home. I touched the hood of the car to see if it was warm. Cold. He hadn't left. That meant he never made it to work and that meant I was in trouble. I was sure Nathan Collins had called him and told him everything I had said. His loyalty was to Dad, not me.

The house was quiet. In a normal person's house, the quiet would be a good thing. In my house, quiet was dangerous. Quiet meant my father was waiting to pounce on me, like the time he beat me for tracking down my mother.

To get this over with quickly, I called out for him. No answer. I made sure to take my shoes off neatly and place them on the shoe rack by the door in the mudroom, not like the last time when I got the belt. Because I always got yelled at for leaving my backpack on the floor, I carried it with me as I made my way through the house, my pulse racing, my muscles firing in small bursts.

He was still here. There was a bottle of aspirin, and various other things he used to chase away a hangover, sitting on the table. His slippers were in front of his favorite chair. Where was he? Was he hiding in another room, waiting for me to walk by so he could attack?

Then I heard the toilet flush upstairs. He must have been paying the price for the night before, which meant he would be in a worse mood.

I climbed the stairs one step at a time, my ears trained for sounds of his presence. I told myself nothing was going to happen. I had nothing to worry about.

He threw open the door just as I was about to pass the bathroom, grabbed the shoulder straps on my backpack, and pushed me up against the wall. He pressed his mouth to my ear. "What do you think you're doing?"

His breath smelled of sour alcohol and vomit.

Gagging, I turned my face away from his. "Going to my room."

He jerked me across the hall and slammed me against the other wall. My head hit hard, but I didn't flinch. His eyes were wide with rage. "Don't be stupid. I know what you did, what you said. With Rachel. With Nathan. What the fuck do you think you're doing, Christa?" He lifted his hand in the air and slapped me, knocking me to the floor.

I curled up in a fetal position and covered my head with my arms. "You killed Eden." He kicked my backside. Luckily my backpack fell off my shoulders, protecting me from the blow, but something inside the pocket cracked. "You don't remember anything from that night, do you?" He kicked me again, this time catching my shin, probably trying to ruin my chances of running ever again. "You killed her, Dad. The police know."

196

In mid-kick, he stopped. "What are you talking about?" He was out of breath, but he stopped kicking me and that was all I could really hope for.

I eased my arm from over my head. He stood over me, breathing heavily, eyeing me like he was waiting for me to talk. "You went out that night, don't you remember?"

"What night?"

"Saturday night. I was in bed by 9:30, and I remember waking up a little later because I heard the garage door open." I pushed myself up from the floor and sat back against the wall. "Don't you remember?"

The expression on his face was a glorious mix of worry and paranoia and utter terror. He didn't remember anything, and at that one moment I had all the power.

"They have the bracelet you gave her." The color drained from his face. It was awesome. "Why did you give her the bracelet you gave to me on my birthday?"

He shook his head and started to walk away. "I didn't give her that bracelet."

"Then how did she get it?"

"I don't know." He stammered and stuttered and paced the floor. "Tell me what happened that night. Tell me why I can't remember what you're talking about."

"You went to the movies that day with someone. Do you remember that much?" This was so much fun. "I had dinner waiting for you when you came home. Do you remember that?"

"Yeah, I remember the movie, and I remember the chicken was good." Dad was growing more and more agitated. "What happened after that?"

"I went upstairs to do my homework and fell asleep by 9:30. I woke up a little later, and I saw you pulling out of the garage. Do you remember that?"

My father narrowed his eyes in concentration. "No."

"You came home a couple of hours later and went straight to bed. The next morning you woke me up to tell me Mrs. Rhodes was here. You even said something about the mud tracked through the house. You made me clean it up. I can't believe you don't remember any of this."

His mouth dropped open. I waited for the light in his brain to go on. This was probably one of the greatest moments of my life, but I wasn't done.

"And what about the baby?" In his drunken stupor, he acknowledged that he had forgotten about the baby, but I couldn't trust him when he was drunk. He always said off the wall things when he was drunk. "Dad, that baby was yours."

As if by flipping a switch, my father changed right before my eyes. He became more alert. The worry left his face. He squared his shoulders and sucked in his gut. "Go to your room," he said, calmly.

The doorbell rang. My father went to the window in his bedroom to see who was outside. He came out of his room looking white as a sheet. "Dammit." He dragged his fingers through his hair and raced downstairs to answer the door. While he did that, I sneaked a peek out the window to find Detective Gonzales and his partner standing on the porch.

Twenty

I huddled out of sight at the top of the stairs and listened. Unless they asked to speak with me specifically, I wasn't going down there. Dad would have to sweat this one out on his own.

"Mr. Pierce, how are you?" Detective Gonzales had an edge to his voice. "This is my partner, Detective Naylor. We'd like to talk with you for a bit."

"It's Dr. Pierce. I'm not feeling very well at the moment. Can we do this later?"

"It won't take long."

"I'd rather save it for another day. You understand, don't you?"

"Well, no, I don't understand. A girl has been brutally murdered, and your family knew her. You can either talk to me now or come down to the station. I can assure you, it would be better if we speak here. People talk, you see. They see things. They whisper. You understand, don't you?"

This guy was tough, badass even. My father was pinned against the wall and couldn't fight back, figuratively speaking. I'd waited my whole life for something like this, for someone to put him in his place, and as much as I would have loved to have been downstairs to see it happen, I settled for listening to it unfold.

"Detective Gonzales?" My father said his name like he was asking a question. "I'm not familiar with that name. I'm good friends with a lot of the police force in this town, but you must be new. How long have you been a detective here?"

"Save it, Mr.—"

"Doctor—"

"Like I was saying, Dr. Pierce, I may be new here, but I didn't just graduate from the criminal justice program."

Well, well, well, my father, the man who always bragged about having the police in his back pocket, had finally met his match.

Dad grumbled. "What do you want? I was getting ready to run to the doctor's office."

"Do they have some new hangover cures that I don't know about at the doctor's office?"

"That's funny. A real comedian. Have a seat."

"Let's start at the beginning. Where were you on Saturday night between nine o'clock and twelve o'clock?"

"I was here. I came home from the movies, had dinner, and was in the rest of the night. I had a glass of wine after dinner and watched a movie."

"And your daughter can verify this?"

"Of course. She was upstairs doing homework."

"On a Saturday night?" Detective Naylor said, sarcastically. "She's a teenager. Shouldn't she be out with friends getting into trouble at the mall?"

"My daughter's different. She's at the head of her class."

Uh-oh. Here we go. Since he was still pissed off at me, I didn't have any hope that he'd defend me.

"What movie?" she asked.

"Movie?" my father said.

"Yes, what movie did you watch?"

Dad stammered. "I fell asleep. I don't remember."

"Do you know anything about a bracelet?" Detective Gonzales asked, impatiently.

"What kind of bracelet?"

"Here's a picture to refresh your memory. You'll notice that on the back it says "For My Princess." Do you know anything about it?"

There was a long silence before Dad said anything. "It looks like the bracelet I gave my daughter on her birthday."

"What was it doing on the victim's body?"

Dad cleared his throat. "You would have to ask my daughter that question."

I almost sprinted down the steps and protested but decided to wait it out a little longer to see if he'd dig himself in further and if the detective would give him an extra shovel.

"But she told us you had taken it back from her."

He laughed. "Why would I do that? It was a present for her birthday."

"Are you saying your daughter's lying?"

"She's been known to lie."

"Why would she lie about something like that?"

I flew down the steps. "Yeah, why would I lie about something like that?"

My father shot up out of the chair. "Get back upstairs and let me handle this."

"No, let her stay," Detective Gonzales said. "Now, where were we? The bracelet. She said you took it back from her, and you're saying she's lying. One of you is lying, and I want to know the truth."

"What I said to you at the police station this morning was the truth." I gave my father a hard stare. "If you don't believe me, call my stepmother, Rachel, because she was there."

"Christa, I said let me handle this." He took a deep breath and sat down again, smoothing the creases out of his pants. "All right, I did take it back from her, but I don't know how Eden got it. I noticed some things missing from my room after she left our house. It's very possible she could've taken it when no one was looking. She was *that type of girl*, if you know what I mean."

Detective Naylor made a tsking sound. "We know what you mean. Coincidentally, your lawyer said the same thing."

Detective Gonzales turned to me. "Is any of this true?"

I didn't know how to answer. My father had already called me a liar. A seed of doubt was already planted. If I said it was true, that meant I would be

203

carrying on with his lie. If I said it wasn't true, I'd never hear the end of it. "Eden wasn't that type of girl. Her mother was raising her on her own after her father left them."

"That doesn't answer the question."

I looked to my father. "She didn't steal the bracelet."

My father tapped his fingers on the arm of the chair.

"So, you're saying your father is lying. I'm not sure I know who to believe. I'm beginning to think both of you are lying."

Shit. That wasn't supposed to happen. "I was always with Eden when she was here. We always studied downstairs. She only spent the night once and was never alone."

"You couldn't have watched her every second she was here." My father laughed as he spoke, trying to make me look like the liar, no doubt. The look in his eyes said he was seething with rage.

"Ask Rachel. She was here every time Eden was. Most of the time I was at her house because my dad doesn't like me having people over."

My father got up out of the chair slowly, his lips pressed tight and the muscles in his jaw clenched. "All right, that's enough. If you wish to speak with me, you'll have to do it through my lawyer. Let me get you his card."

"Don't bother. We know who he is." The two detectives stood to leave. "One more question. Mr. Excuse me. Dr. Pierce, what kind of car do you drive?"

"Out!"

"By the way, that clock on the mantel is three hours behind the others."

I whipped my head around to the clock on the mantel. My knees almost gave out from under me. I forgot to turn one of the clocks back to the original time on the night I killed Eden. "Oh, it's probably from the time change."

"Three hours, though?" Detective Gonzales jutted his chin and narrowed his eyes. "You'll be seeing us again."

Once they were in their car, Dad slammed the door shut, locked it, and turned to face me. I knew what was coming. Before he had a chance to make his move, I was up the stairs and locked in my bedroom, pushing my desk in front of the door. He slammed himself against the door, screaming my name. "You better open up right now."

"Go away." I reached in the pocket of my backpack for my mother's cell phone. It was broken. That was the cracking noise I'd heard when he kicked me.

"This is my house." He pounded on the door so hard it shook everything on my desk. "Open this fucking door. Now."

"You killed my friend. I'm afraid you're going to kill me, too." Quickly, I pulled out my phone and called Rachel. She didn't answer, but I left a message. "I'm locked in my room. Dad is trying to kill me. Send help."

"Who are you talking to? You better not be calling anyone."

"You're scaring me."

My father continued pounding on the door, screaming and swearing. "If I break this door or my hand, you're going to get it."

"Why did you kill Eden?"

"I didn't kill her."

"Then where did you go that night?" I knew that would shut him up for a minute.

At this point, I didn't have anything to lose, so I called my mother on my cell phone. She wouldn't recognize the number, so I had no hope that she'd answer the call. I left the same message with her that I had left Rachel. Now all I had to do was wait it out until someone came to my rescue. Until then, I provoked him a little more.

"Is it a coincidence that the last person to see Eden alive was driving a car like yours?"

"What are you up to, Christa?" His mouth was pressed against the door—the volume of his voice sounding as if he were in the room with me.

"What are *you* up to, Dad? I know you were messing around with her."

Silence.

Then he slammed into the door again, pushing the desk back an inch or two. In case he broke the door down, I locked myself in the closet, with my phone at the ready. The next step was to call 9-1-1.

Twenty-one

Over the next few hours, my father pounded on the door less and only yelled instead of screaming in rage, but I stayed locked in the closet for safety. It was another barrier he'd have to break through to get to me.

No word from my mother or Rachel. My mother I could understand because she didn't know my phone number. Rachel, on the other hand, should have picked up the call, unless she was still mad at me for the other day. She seemed more than angry; she was hateful. If someone didn't come to my rescue soon, I'd have to face my father when I stepped foot outside my bedroom door, and I would get worse than the belt.

After a while, Dad stopped pounding on the door altogether. It was getting late. I was hungry and had to pee. I inched out of the closet and listened for sounds of his presence outside the door. The house was quiet. The TV wasn't on so I knew he wasn't downstairs. I didn't want to take a chance of running into him on my way to the bathroom, so I emptied the trashcan to relieve myself. Before I could even spill the trash onto the floor, I heard police sirens blaring from far away. At first, I thought it might have been just another accident down at the crazy intersection near the school, but the sirens grew louder. And louder. More than one police car, for sure. Down on the road outside our housing development. Two streets over. In my driveway. I could hear Dad scrambling around in the hallway outside my door.

The detectives left hours ago. What more did they want from us so soon? My room faced the back yard so I couldn't see what was going on, but I could hear a frantic-voiced Detective Gonzales pounding on the front door, shouting he had a warrant to search the house.

No, no, no, no! This wasn't supposed to happen yet. I broke out in a cold sweat. I figured they'd come, planned on it, hoped for it, but not yet. Not yet.

I pushed my desk out of the way and opened the door a crack, just enough to hear what was going on downstairs.

"We have a warrant to search everything on the premises, Dr. Pierce," Detective Gonzales said.

"Not until I speak with my lawyer."

"Call him while we search. Now, if you don't mind, step out of the way."

I listened as the detective gave instructions to the other officers. One was to go in the garage, another to my father's office, and the others upstairs. Their hurried feet stomped up the steps and went into the many spare bedrooms. Rachel always had all the beds dressed and ready to go as if we were expecting overnight guests.

What a joke. Dad never let anyone in the house, except the women he screwed.

I watched the police from my bedroom doorway. They looked like ants, tunneling back and forth.

The next thing I knew, Detective Gonzales was marching upstairs, heading straight toward me. "Is this your room?"

I nearly choked. "Yes."

"Could you step out of the way, please? I have a warrant."

"Christa, get down here," Dad yelled from downstairs. "Now."

"It might be a good idea to listen to him."

As I walked downstairs, I wondered which was worse: facing my father after our little standoff or the police going through my things—not that there was anything that could implicate me in there. The thought of it was still unnerving, though.

My father was on the phone, pacing back and forth, his face red with anger. If he kept this up, he'd have a heart attack. I could only wish. As soon as he saw me, he took a swing at my face. I jumped out of the way and crashed into the hall table, knocking a vase to the floor. Shards of ceramic scattered all over the foyer.

Detective Naylor poked her head out of Dad's office, wide-eyed and curious. "Is there a problem out here?"

"She tripped," my father said before I had a chance to speak. "She's going to clean it up now. Aren't you, Christa?"

209

No, I wasn't. I stayed where I was, watching all this unfold.

"Naylor," someone yelled. "Can you come in the garage for a second?"

"Be right there."

Phone still pressed to his ear, Dad gave me a look that normally would have made me shiver. I should have been pissing my pants with fear, but I was too busy listening to what was going on in the garage.

"Dr. Pierce," Detective Naylor called from the garage. "Could you come here, please?"

"You stay put and keep your mouth shut," Dad said through clenched teeth. "You run your mouth like you did earlier, you can kiss your ass goodbye. I'll cut you off so fast, you'll be out on the streets to fend for yourself. Don't expect help from your mother either."

Quietly, I followed him out to the garage, hiding behind the door, listening.

"What can I help you with?" Dad's voice actually quivered.

I peeked through the crack and saw Naylor holding up the tire iron I used to hit Eden over the head. "There's blood on here."

"That could be from the stain I used on the deck last year." He tried to act nonchalant about it, but it came out as a nervous laugh.

"Don't they provide stir-sticks at home improvement stores nowadays?"

"This was one of those big five-gallon containers."

"This car matches the description of the one that picked the victim up on the night of the murder." Naylor was so cool and calm about the whole thing.

"I'm sure there are a number of cars like mine."

"Not one with a bloody tire iron in the trunk."

"My lawyer is going to hear about this."

Before I could catch my breath, Detective Gonzales breezed by me, carrying the bag I had stuffed at the back of Dad's closet. "Is this yours?" he said to Dad.

"I haven't seen that thing in ages."

"Really? Would you like to know what I found in here?"

"Probably nothing since I haven't used it in close to five years."

Detective Gonzales carefully pulled out a pair of blood-stained pants and a jacket. "Look familiar?"

Dad's face went white.

"By the way, what's your middle name?"

"James." He gulped. "Why?"

"Michael James Pierce?"

Dad cleared his throat. "Yes."

"You have a nice collection of button-down Oxford's embroidered with your initials."

"Is there a law against that?"

"No, but it just so happens that the baby was wrapped in one with the initials MJP on the pocket."

My father squirmed. "I'm sure there are lots of people out there with those same initials."

"Excuse me, Detective G," a young officer said. He held up a picture and one of our kitchen knives side-by-side. "It looks like they match."

"That's good enough for me. Michael Pierce, you're under arrest for the murder of Eden Rhodes." Detective Gonzales proceeded to read him his Miranda rights as one of the cops took his phone away from him and put handcuffs on him. "Get him out of here."

"What are you doing?" I pretended to protest.

"Arresting him," Detective Gonzales said. "We'll be done in a while. In the meantime, why don't you take a seat."

I walked to the living room, tip-toeing around the shards of broken ceramic on the floor. The detective followed. "I'm not answering any questions without a lawyer present." The words came out of my mouth before I could stop them. What a dumb thing to say.

"I'm not asking any. I expect you'll be at the station before long anyway."

What did he mean by that?

"Who's here to take care of you?"

"I'm old enough to take care of myself."

"Where's your stepmother?"

"Gone."

He didn't respond, only flipped through his notebook. "Naylor? Can you call this number and ask the stepmom to get here as soon as possible?"

She looked over his shoulder and dialed the number before walking away. As hard as I tried, I could barely make out what she was saying. It was especially hard when Detective Gonzales studied me like I was a specimen under a microscope.

His stare unnerved me. "What?" I said, finally.

He shrugged. "Nothing. As soon as your stepmother gets here, I'll need to see you at the station. We have a lot of things to talk about."

"I tried that, remember?"

He sat on the couch, elbows resting on his knees. A smile worked across his face as his eyes narrowed.

"Maybe I'll go up to my room and get out of your way."

"Maybe you'll sit here until we're done."

Detective Naylor came into the living room, rubbing her lower back. "They're still working on the car."

"How long before the stepmom arrives?"

"No answer. I'll keep trying."

"All right. Head back to the station and get him settled in. I'll keep an eye on this one for a while."

My gut rumbled from nerves. If I stayed there much longer, I feared I'd lose control of all bodily functions. "Can I at least go to the bathroom?"

"Is there one downstairs?"

I pointed over my shoulder toward the hallway. "The powder room."

"Fine."

I turned the fan on in the bathroom and locked the door. Finally, a moment to myself. I braced myself against the sink, the muscles in my arms twitching, cramping. My head spun.

Killing Eden was the easy part. Getting away with it was proving harder. I had to get out of here, and once the cops left, I could do that. Unless Rachel showed up. She may not even care enough to answer the calls, so I'd worry about her when I needed to worry about her. I had to hold on for a little longer until the cops left. But wait a minute. What was I thinking? I was alone with a detective for once—no lawyer, no Rachel, no one to stop me from telling him everything.

Out in the living room, Detective Gonzales was swiping through his phone. "Have a seat."

I sat on the edge of Dad's favorite chair.

"Are you going to be okay?"

Policemen carried boxes and envelopes filled with who knows what from the house. The sight of it made me tense. "I've always seen this type of thing on television. It's very different when it happens to you. I feel violated."

"TV drama ain't real life. So, do you want to talk about anything?"

I stared at my feet before looking at him. "You look at me like I know something."

He smiled thinly. "I think you know a lot." His expression softened. "How long has this been going on?"

I looked to the left and to the right, unsure of what he was asking. "How long has what been going on?"

"You don't have to be afraid anymore. I understand what you're going through."

I gritted my teeth as I dug my nails into the leather on the arms of the chair. "Nobody understands what I'm going through."

"I understand more than you know."

"Do you really now?"

He looked away and cleared his throat. "It helps to talk."

He wanted to know all about my abusive home life? Fine. I'd tell him everything. Remembering the way I had tricked myself into crying many times since Eden's death, I tried it again. First, I squeezed my eyes shut, then I quivered my chin and bottom lip, and before I knew it, tears.

"It seems like you have it pretty rough." His voice was awkwardly sympathetic for a tough guy. It confused me. Other than my mother, no one had ever spoken to me like that.

I wiped the fake tears away with my thumb. "Yeah, I guess so." Then something weird happened. My eyes burned with tears without even trying. My throat tightened, not because I was afraid or tense. It was hard to swallow, hard to talk, but I talked. Words flowed freely out of my mouth like the tears in my eyes. I said things I never knew I wanted to say. This was real. "He kept my mother away for me. Did you know that?"

"I didn't."

"I tracked her down, though. And when I came home from finding her, he beat me with a belt."

He took out his pen and notepad. "When was this?"

"I don't remember the exact day."

"What else has he done recently?"

"He slapped me because he thought I hacked into his phone."

"Why would he think you hacked into his phone?"

"I know, right?" I got up and searched for a box of tissues. For the first time in my life, I unleashed what I had bottled up for years. It helped that the detective was eating it all up. Since I was sharing all my long-held secrets, and he was hanging on every word, I figured I'd keep going. It could only help me build a case against Dad. "He was sleeping with her, you know."

The detective cocked his head to the side and stared up at me. "He was sleeping with who?"

"Eden."

His eyes grew wide as he fell back against the couch like someone pinned him there. "Are you sure?"

"I heard them."

"Heard them how, when?"

I sat in my father's chair again. I liked knowing I was in close proximity to one of his favorite things while I destroyed him sentence by sentence. I felt like a queen sitting on the throne of her defeated foe. "A couple of months ago we—"

"We? Who's we?"

"Eden and I had gone to visit him at his office on campus. I went out for a coffee run, and when I came back, I heard noises inside."

"What kind of noises?"

"Sex noises. Moaning, heavy breathing."

"You realize what you're saying, right?"

"Of course, I do."

"Can I ask you about the bracelet and get the truth now?"

"What I told you was true. If you ask Rachel, she'll confirm what happened that night at my birthday dinner. I opened the box, I complained about it, he heard me, he took it back. I should've kept my mouth shut, but I was tired of being called Princess. If he thought I was such a princess, why did he beat me?"

The detective gestured that he understood. "Can you confirm his whereabouts on the night of the murder?"

I took a deep breath. This guy was eating right out of my hands, lapping it up like a stupid, hungry dog. "I fell asleep around 9:30 or so. The sound of his car starting and the garage door opening and closing woke me up not long after. You see, my bedroom is within earshot of the garage, so I can always hear when someone comes and goes. He left for a couple of hours and that's all I remember."

"Do you remember what time he came home?"

"I don't. He woke me up the next morning and told me Eden's mom was downstairs looking for her."

"Did you notice anything strange about his behavior?"

"Yes, he kept saying he didn't remember anything about the night before. He didn't even remember tracking mud through the house. After Eden's mom left, he made me vacuum the floors."

"Mud? Where's the vacuum?"

"In the pantry, off the kitchen."

Detective Gonzales stood up without another word and went straight for the closet. He called for one of his officers and asked him to take the vacuum cleaner for evidence. While he did that, I stifled a giggle. This guy was so gullible, feeling sorry for the poor little abused girl, falling for her sob story, believing every pathetic word.

"All right, is there anything else I should know?"

"I can't think of anything else."

"I just have a couple more questions." His cell phone rang. "One minute while I take this. This is G. Whatcha got?"

I could hear a woman's voice. The detective nodded his head and mumbled some things while he listened. The phone call was short.

"It looks like we can't reach your stepmother. Speaking of which, what's going on there?"

"When she found out about Eden, she left him."

"You mean she knows, too?"

"She knows. When you talk to her, though, don't expect the truth."

"Why do you say that?"

"For some reason, she defends him. Even after everything that's happened. I don't know why."

"Was he abusive to her as well?"

"He's pushed her around a few times, but he's been cheating on her since as long as I can remember."

He closed his little notebook and shoved it in his jacket pocket. "Are you going to be okay by yourself?"

"I'll be fine. It'll sink in later, and I'll want to be by myself. To process things."

"I understand. Here's my card. If you need me, call. I'll probably have a patrol swing by the neighborhood to see if everything is okay. I know it's tough, but once you get away from…this, you'll see there's a beautiful world out there."

This guy seemed to be one of those touchy-feely types. As long as I had him on the line, I'd keep reeling him in. "Is that why you became a detective, to protect people like me?"

"I like putting the bad guys away." His eyes flashed a hint of something. "We'll keep trying to get in touch with your stepmother. In the meantime, lock up, stay safe." He rounded up his team and headed for the door. He stood there and watched his men and women get back in their vehicles before turning back to me. "I lied. I do have one more question."

"Sure."

"Why do you know so much about what your father has been doing?"

I laughed nervously. "We live in the same house. How wouldn't I know?"

"I mean, you seem to have all the details while he has none. Why is that?"

The blood drained from my face so fast I was sure he saw the physical reaction. "Ask him."

"Oh, I will. Do me a favor. Don't go anywhere. When your stepmother gets here, I would like to see both of you at the police station."

"Tonight?"

"Tomorrow. You had a traumatic experience. You should rest. Don't be alarmed when you see the patrol car driving around the neighborhood. Have a nice evening, Ms. Pierce."

Twenty-two

After the police cleared out, I walked from room-to-room straightening up some of the mess they left behind: drawers open, papers scattered, clothes strewn about, closet doors left hanging open. Like we had been robbed. Even if I wanted this to happen, I felt violated somehow. After a while, I realized I was all alone. No Dad. No Rachel. No rules. No worries.

The house was quiet, empty, and all mine. No one could stop me from blasting music or watching whatever I wanted on TV. I could go to bed late, run around the house naked, and eat a gallon of ice cream if I wanted. I was free. For the first time, I wasn't afraid of being in my own house. I let out a yelp and ran the halls, laughing.

I bounced up and down on Dad's bed, kicking the covers onto the floor, making an even bigger mess than what the police left behind. All the hairs on my body stood up, I was so happy. I had never felt such freedom.

Out of breath, I flopped onto the bed and howled like a wolf. Nobody could stop me. I'd pulled it off. I couldn't believe it. I had pulled it off. Dad was going to jail, and I was free of him forever. I laughed so hard my cheeks hurt.

The look on his face when Detective Gonzales said he was under arrest was the best thing I had ever seen. I wished I had taken a picture of that moment to have it forever cemented in history, uploading it to the internet for everyone to see, point at, laugh at.

Once I stopped laughing, I raided the kitchen. I made a batch of chocolate chip cookies. Way at the back of the freezer, I found a frozen pizza. That went into the oven, too. Anything I wasn't normally allowed to eat went in my mouth.

By midnight, I was in front of the TV, streaming a movie and moaning, unable to move from eating so much. I couldn't remember when I finally fell asleep.

Stomach cramps woke me up in the morning. I thought a soak in the bathtub would make me feel better. As the water filled the tub, I blasted music in my room. The sound filled the house, and I found myself cringing at the strangeness of it all. I was never allowed to listen to music above a whisper and here it was feeling like front row seats at a concert. This was the greatest finger flip I could imagine, next to succeeding at framing Dad.

The water seeped over the top of the tub as I climbed in. I propped my feet up and leaned back, singing off key as loud as I could without straining a vocal cord. This was relaxing. I was relaxed. The feeling was so foreign to me. I'd never lived a moment of my life where I wasn't anticipating a blow from that man.

The bath did the trick on my bloated belly. I wrapped a towel around me and opened the door. Rachel stood in the hallway, leaning against the wall, arms crossed, scowling. Her hair was a mess, her makeup was all smudged, and she was still in pajamas. With my father out of her life, maybe she'd decided to let herself go. The last time I saw her, she didn't look that well either.

"Are you all right?" I could tell by the tone of her voice that she didn't really care how I was.

"In shock. My head is spinning."

"Is that why you were singing in the tub?"

Busted. "I'm not feeling well."

"What happened last night?"

"What do you think happened?"

"I'm not in the mood."

"Dad was arrested. His car matched the description in the surveillance video, and they found a gym bag full of bloody clothes in his closet."

Her mouth dropped open. "There has to be some mistake. He wouldn't do something like that."

"I can't believe after all this time you're still defending him. You even said yourself that he was cruel."

"Cruel is one thing. Killing someone is a stretch."

I didn't understand this woman. My father cheated on her, abused her, abused me in front of her, and yet she couldn't admit how awful he was. I went to my closet to dress. "Well, apparently it's not that much of a stretch."

Rachel followed me into my room. "You don't seem upset about any of this."

"I had a long couple of days. I'm in shock. I'm still trying to digest it." I pulled out a pair of loose-fitting jeans and a sweatshirt. "A bunch of cops searched the house and put handcuffs on Dad yesterday. How do you expect me to act?"

She threw her hands up. "Hysterical. Bawling your eyes out. Frantic. I don't know. You tell me."

"Why aren't you hysterical or bawling your eyes out considering your husband is going to jail for murder?"

"Don't turn this around on me."

"Whatever." I turned to walk away. "You never should've come back."

"Where do you think you're going?"

I threw my arms out to the side. "Look at this place. I'd like to clean it up. You can help me instead of standing there with your thumb up your ass."

"You can do that later. We have to go downtown. Everyone is waiting for you."

The stomach cramps I had earlier that morning came back with a vengeance at the thought of being trapped at the police station again. I wasn't going anywhere with her.

"Finish getting ready. While you do, I have another question." Rachel sat on my bed, cocky, bold. "I can understand you hate your father because of the way he treated you."

"Terrorized me."

"Semantics."

"You lived it, too."

"There's something I can't understand."

When she didn't continue, I asked, "And what is that?"

"Eden meant a lot to you, didn't she? Where are the tears for her?"

"Just because you haven't seen them, doesn't mean they aren't there."

Rachel kicked her leg back and forth. There was a defiant look in her eyes, one that I hadn't seen before. She didn't scare me, but this was entertaining. "It really must've bothered you, didn't it?"

I sat at my desk to put my socks on. "What are you talking about?"

"When you were a little girl, you did anything and everything to get your father's attention, his love, his approval."

Rachel was working hard at pushing my buttons. She'd never talked to me like this before. "What are you getting at?"

"It must've eaten away at you to watch him give his attention and, inappropriate though it was, affection to your best friend. How did that make you feel?"

I burst out laughing. "Are you in therapy? Are you picking up some pointers from your new doctor?"

"It must've killed you to know he was kinder to her than he ever was to you."

"Are we talking about me or are we talking about you? I could throw those same questions back at you, you know."

"I stopped loving your father a long time ago. The little act I put on when he would go out and screw around or even bring them here in the house? That was all for show. That act was me being angry I didn't have the money to leave. I felt trapped, but I wasn't hurt by his actions. And for your information, I was sickened when I found out about Eden. But how did that make *you* feel, Christa?"

Thankfully, her phone rang. Not taking her eyes off me to look at the number on the screen, she took the call. "Hello? Yes, I know. I'm trying, but she's fighting me."

"Who are you talking to? Don't tell them that." I jumped off the chair and lunged toward her. "Who is it?"

Rachel held her arm out to block me from snatching the phone. "I'll have her there within half an hour." She ended the call and stared at me. "That was that slimeball Nathan Collins. He's getting impatient, so get your shoes on. I'll drive you."

"Why don't you go home? I can drive myself." I started to walk away, but she took hold of my arm and pulled me back. "Let go of me." I pushed her backwards onto the bed.

She flopped around like a fish on the ground until she got oriented. "I told you to finish getting dressed. Hurry up and let's go. I'm not leaving without you."

"The only way I'm going to get in that car with you is if you drag me out by my hair. I'm not going anywhere. Do you understand? So, get out of my room, and get out of this house."

As I turned to hold the door open for her, something flew at the back of my head. I recoiled at the impact. Her purse lay on the floor at my feet.

"I told you. Get in the car."

I snatched the purse from the floor and threw it at her face as hard as I could. The edge of the purse hit her square on the nose. She shrieked and fell backwards onto the floor. Blood gushed from her nose like a faucet on full blast. "And I told you, no."

"Are you going to kill me like you killed Eden?"

I froze. I couldn't will my body to take another breath. The question hit me like a bullet.

"You won't get away with this."

Rachel had no problem ratting me out to my dad, so she'd do it in a nano-second to the police. Lucky for me, she was busy wiping blood off her face and couldn't see me struggling with her accusation.

What did she know? Nothing. She didn't know anything. She wasn't even here that night.

I shook my head rapidly, forcing myself out of the stupor. "What are you talking about?" I said as calmly as I could pretend.

"Come on, don't play dumb. That's my gig. You know what you did."

"What if I did kill her? What are you going to do about it?"

Even through the tears and the blood running down her face, I could see the horror in her eyes.

Shit!

What had I done? She pushed my buttons, and I fell for it. I fell for her stupid trick and confessed. She didn't really think I'd done it and was only messing with me.

"I was only playing. I don't think you killed her." She inched backwards away for me. I didn't realize I was walking toward her." Did you?"

"Fight me."

"What?"

"Stand up and fight me. I don't want this to be easy."

"I always thought there was something wrong with you. You were probably the most unfeeling little girl I had ever met in my life. You're psycho."

I threw my head back and laughed. "Did you learn that by watching Dr. Phil?"

"What's wrong with you? All right, you win. Just go. I'll tell them you ran away."

"You won't tell them anything." Before I could even stop myself, I punched Rachel in the face. She fell backwards, knocking her head off the wall and sliding to the floor, passed out.

She had it coming. Plus, she knew what I did. Even if she was pushing my buttons, the seed of doubt was in her head. She could plant that seed in the heads of the police, and I couldn't have that. I had to protect myself. This was a matter of survival.

I shoved a few things in a bag and grabbed the money I had stashed in the closet. I had about $500 saved up. I dumped all my school books onto the floor and filled my backpack up with food so I wouldn't have to stop anywhere.

The police would be on the lookout for Dad's car, but mine was still here. Normally, my car keys were hanging in the mudroom by the garage. Not this time. Gone. My damn keys were gone. He must have hidden them.

I searched the kitchen and the living room frantically but couldn't find them anywhere. If I didn't hurry, Rachel would wake up or the police would come to the house and drag me to the station. Rachel's car. No one would be looking for her car until after she woke up and blabbed her mouth. I dug through her purse and came up empty for the car keys. I felt around in her jacket pocket and found them.

I ran to the car and took off. All I knew I was heading toward Ohio to be with Mom. I had no idea where I was going because she hadn't given me her new address yet and still hadn't answered my call. It was a long drive. I still had to pass through most of New York and a little part of Pennsylvania before I even hit the border. That gave me enough time to call until she answered her phone.

Unfortunately, Rachel's car was almost out of gas. No way could I stop to fill up until I was out of the area. Thanks to adrenaline, I couldn't keep the car on the road, I was shaking so badly. My heart pumped harder than when I ran. The feeling was same but different. This time I wasn't running toward a finish line; I was running away.

This wasn't how I imagined any of it happening. I expected them to arrest my father and book him for the murder of his lover, Eden Rhodes. And that was going to be the end of that. Since he couldn't remember anything that happened that night, he wouldn't be able to defend himself. I'd continue to point the finger at him. I would tell the police of the atrocities that went on in our house. I'd tell them how he hit his only daughter, how he mentally tortured her, and how he verbally abused her. I'd tell them he was messing around with young girls. My father was a monster, and this was the only way to stop him for good.

It wouldn't be long before someone called Rachel's phone and wondered where she was, before somebody stopped at the house and found her body lying there, before she woke up and started running her mouth, before someone reported her car stolen and figured out I was the person who stole it. It wouldn't be long before someone reported me as a runaway

I had to stop for gas somewhere. The needle was on E. I drummed my fingers on the steering wheel nervously as I scanned the highway for signs of a convenience store. A few miles along the road, I finally saw a large sign for a gas station hovering above the trees like a beacon on a hill.

After getting off the exit ramp, I pulled over and put on a nondescript gray hoodie, baggy enough to conceal my face and hide the fact that I was a girl.

There was one snag in all of this, and it was a big one. All gas pumps were pre-pay, and I only had cash. I was smart enough to know not to use my credit card, at least. But how was I going to go into the store and ask to fill up the tank without being seen on the surveillance video? I had no choice. It was either fill up the tank or walk the rest of the way to Ohio.

I kept the hoodie on and put on a pair of sunglasses. As casual as possible, I strolled into the store. "I need to fill up."

"Which pump?" the scruffy looking older woman behind the counter said, not bothering to look up.

"Pump two."

"I need your driver's license, please."

"Why?"

"So you don't drive off without paying."

"Oh, um, I left it in the car. How about this? I'll give you fifty bucks and if it's less than that, you can keep the change."

"We're not allowed to accept tips."

It just so happened there was a container for a fundraiser for a young cancer patient in the area. I held up the container, rattling the coins inside. "Then you can put the change in here. Sound good?"

She cracked her gum. "Sure. Go ahead. Thanks for the donation."

I waved over my shoulder as I walked out the door. While the gas pumped, I tried to reach my mother again until it was done filling up. She still wasn't answering my calls. Anxious, I jumped back in the car and headed for the highway, not entirely sure where I was going.

Just before I reached Cleveland, my mother called. "Michael, if this is you, I have nothing to say to you. Please stop calling."

"Mom."

"Christa?"

"Listen, I'm on my way to your house. Where do you live?"

"What's going on?"

"I have a lot to tell you, but I can't stay on the phone too long." I had to give her the worst of it so she would take sympathy on me. "Dad and I had a huge fight. He kicked the phone and broke it. Then he got arrested. He murdered my best friend."

Silence. For a brief second, I thought the phone had gone dead.

"Are you there?"

"Yes. A little stunned is all. Why are you coming here?"

That felt like a slap in the face. "I thought you wanted me to come and live with you."

"I do, but if your father got arrested, you should probably stay there until everything clears up."

"Mom, I'm scared. I don't know what to do. I need to get away for a few days to clear my head. I'll go back. I need you right now."

She gave me the address to her house. It was just outside of Columbus.

"I'll let my sister know you're coming. I can't wait to see you. I'll try to have dinner ready for you when you get here. How much longer?"

"Coming up on Cleveland right now."

"That's rather close. When did you leave?"

I didn't want to answer all her questions while I was driving in case I got caught on my phone. "I'll tell you everything when I get there."

"Okay, I'll see you in a few hours."

"Mom, I wish you had raised me instead of him."

"Me, too, honey."

I hung up the phone just in time. A police car rode alongside me for a few seconds. Out of the corner of my eye, I could see the cop watching me. He sped up and passed me, turning his siren on and gunning it. I gripped the steering wheel so hard my knuckles turned white.

Twenty-three

Within five minutes, I passed the trooper while he did a traffic stop along the highway. Not wanting to give him any reason to chase after me, I pulled into the left lane and slowed down. With the officer distracted by his duties, I let out a hefty sigh and dropped my shoulders.

Ten minutes later, he was behind me. I kept my speed at exactly 65 until he got frustrated with my driving and passed me. It took me an hour to stop shaking.

As I got closer to my mother's house, I searched for places to dump Rachel's car. I wanted someplace close enough so I didn't have to run too far but far enough away that it couldn't be traced back to me. A car junkyard would have been perfect, but junkyards didn't show up on the GPS. I couldn't put it someplace where people would notice it right away, so any public place like a school parking lot or library was out of the question.

With only about a mile left to go before I got to my mother's, I gave up searching for a place to dump it and settled on a back alley in a sketchy neighborhood. I parked it next to an abandoned car up on cement blocks.

I gathered all of Rachel's insurance, registration papers, and anything with her name and address on it and shoved it all in a plastic bag, locked the car, and started to walk away. The neighborhood dogs barked. Two of them jumped against the fence that separated their yard from the alley. I side-stepped out of their way in case one of the fences had a hole in it.

I smelled cigarette smoke.

"Where do you think you're going?" Two guys dressed in black walked out from behind a dilapidated garage about ten yards in front of me. I nearly pissed myself.

"Uh, nowhere." I kept my face concealed and tried to lower my voice a couple of registers to make it sound manly. In the dark, with my build, I could definitely pass for a guy.

"Got any money?" one of them said.

"No." I had to get out of there or I was going to lose my life. "I'll be on my way."

"You ain't going nowhere," the other one said.

Think, Christa! "The police are already after me, and if you guys chase me they'll find you faster."

"Oh yeah? What'd you do?"

"I killed someone."

They stepped a few feet closer. They were only teenagers obviously looking for trouble.

"That's messed up," said one.

"You did not," said the other one, walking toward me slowly. Five yards away.

"I have a gun, so step off. I'm already wanted for murder. What's one more dead body?"

"I don't believe you. You ain't even a dude."

I inched backwards. The dogs barked louder. The guys kept walking toward me. I was in a strange town, and I had no idea where to run. It was bitter cold and pitch dark out. My pulse raced, leaving me feeling shaky and squirrely.

"Got any money?"

"I already told you no."

"Sure you do. Look at that car."

"It's not mine. I stole it."

"She stole it but she made sure to lock the door," the one said to the other, smacking his arm. Both guys burst out laughing. "Give us some money, and we won't hurt you."

I didn't have much, but it was all I had to survive on for who knew how long. "You're gonna have to catch me first." I took off in a mad sprint, thinking they weren't going to chase me. Boy, was I wrong. They were fast, almost as fast as I was, but I had a few things going for me that they didn't: training and stamina.

As I ran, I searched for a main road. These guys wouldn't be so willing to chase a girl down a busy street, but after I turned out of the alley, they were still behind me. Cars drove right past us and not a single one stopped to help, beeped a horn, or yelled out the window at them. Maybe this was their neighborhood and everyone knew them, or maybe people didn't care in this part of town. I kept running, not slowing down a bit even though my lungs and legs were on fire.

After a few minutes of a sprinting pace, I heard them give up. I glanced back to find both doubled over in the middle of the street, breathing loud and heavy.

"Next time you won't be so lucky," one shouted.

"Stupid bitch," the other said.

That was close. Too close. To be on the safe side, I kept running until I found a strip mall. I hung out at the side of a fabric store, crouched on the ground, trying to catch my breath. I had memorized the route to my mother's house on the GPS before getting out of the car but now had no idea where I was. I was so, so lost and had no alternative but to use the navigation system on my phone.

Shaking violently, I somehow managed to punch in the address to my aunt's house. I was only half a mile away. It looked like I was a few streets over from Dinkman Avenue, and from there it was a straight shot to the west side. I gave myself a few more minutes to calm down, keeping my ears trained for the jackasses who'd chased me.

Sharp cramps, like a zillion hot needles, shot through my quadriceps as I stood up. I rubbed and stretched and rubbed and stretched some more before I headed out. My legs were like jelly and just a second away from giving out on me altogether.

As I passed garbage cans, I dropped Rachel's important papers inside, spreading them throughout the town. Evidence of who owned the car was now scattered. It wouldn't take the cops long to figure it out once they ran the plates, but I wasn't going to help them along.

When I finally found my aunt's house, I was ready to collapse. Adrenaline was the only thing keeping me going, but the effects were waning.

I rang the doorbell, prompting a dog inside the house to bark. It must have been my aunt's because I didn't see one when I visited my mom. The porch light came on. My mother peeked through a curtain, smiled, and yanked open the door.

"I was worried about you," she said, throwing her arms around me. "You look awful. Come inside."

"Sorry it took so long. The car broke down about a mile from here, and I had to leave it."

"What did you do, run?"

"I had to." I peeled off my shoes and started to place them neatly by the door but stopped myself. This wasn't my father's house, and I wasn't going to live by his rules any longer.

"You should've called. I would've picked you up."

"I didn't want to wake the whole house up."

"It's not that late."

"Who's this little guy?" I bent down to scratch the dog behind the ears, and he bit my hand. "Never mind."

"Down, Stinky. He's an asshole. He hates everyone but my sister. How's your hand?"

"It's fine. Animals never were my thing."

"Are you hungry?" My mother helped the bag off my shoulder. "I made a nice beef stew. Do you like beef stew?"

"I'll eat anything right now."

"My sister works the night shift, so it's just the two of us."

The house was warm. Way too warm. My father kept the house cold, usually at 63°, no matter how cold it was outside, so this felt nice. The house was small and homey, quite different from the showroom of the mini-mansion we lived in. I sat down at the table and watched my mother move around the kitchen. The last time I saw her, she was hunched over a cup of tea at my house, begging for me to run away with her. This was what I would have run away to—a very different life.

"I can't believe you're here. I'm a little unprepared."

"Sorry about that. It just got to be too much."

She pulled out a chair and sat next to me. "Tell me what happened. It sounds juicy and scandalous."

"Dad and I had a fight. I locked myself in my room and tried to call you and Rachel. The next thing I knew, the police were knocking at the door with a search warrant."

"Did you leave a message? Because I saw the number and automatically deleted it."

When the microwave dinged, my mother jumped up and reached inside. The smell of the beef stew made my belly twinge from hunger.

"That was me. He kicked my backpack and broke the phone."

She placed the steaming bowl in front of me and handed me a spoon. "What would you like to drink? I have some hot chocolate."

"That would be great."

I couldn't take my eyes off of her. Kids grow up with their mothers waiting on them, cooking for them, coming to their rescue, but I never had any of that. Would she come to my rescue, protect me from the police?

"Where was Rachel in all of this?"

"She never answered my call."

"Is that normal for her?"

"Not really. She hates me and Dad now. She eventually showed up but only after the police called her and made her come to the house to keep an eye on me."

My mother placed the hot chocolate before me and gave me a look, but I didn't know her well enough to understand what that look meant. "If she showed up, what are you doing here?"

I didn't have an answer.

"Not to say I don't want you here, but…" She closed her eyes and waved a hand. "Never mind."

"I told you I couldn't take it any longer. I had to get away."

A long pause. "I see."

I was curious to know if they were broadcasting what happened all the way over here in Ohio. "Have you been keeping up with the news?"

240

"My old friends have been keeping me up to date." She stared at me over her cup of cocoa. "You know I'm not a fan of your father's, but I have a hard time believing he would kill someone. Hire someone else to do it? Sure."

"Really, why?

"He's too much of a coward."

"Then who could it be?"

"My sister and I have been talking about it a lot. It seems to me that whoever did it was close to the girl. Very close."

I stirred the potatoes and carrots around, unable to look her in the eye. "She was seeing someone named Kyle for a while. But then I told you he was fooling around with her, Dad was."

"That doesn't surprise me, but I still don't think it was him."

It seemed like she had some inside information that I hadn't heard about. "Whoever it was got her pregnant."

"It couldn't have been your father, then. He can't have any more children."

Rachel mentioned the vasectomy. At the time, I thought she was lying to protect him. With my mother's confirmation, I knew she had to be telling the truth because she wouldn't defend him. That most definitely wasn't his baby. I did this for nothing. Dad wasn't going to jail for life for Eden's death. "I don't feel so well."

"I imagine not." There was that look in her eye again. "I imagine you feel quite sick about everything. I imagine you need someone to talk to."

"Everything is happening so fast. It's hard to keep up. Maybe I'll feel better tomorrow. I'm exhausted."

"You can sleep in my bed, and I'll sleep on the couch. It's only a single bed, but it'll do. It's really comfortable. Give me a hug."

Even as tall as I was, I felt so small in her arms. "What do you think our life would've been like if you and Dad never got divorced?"

"We would've been miserable, but at least we would've been together and I could have done right by you." She cradled my face in her hands. "Things would be different now, that's for sure."

"What do you mean?"

"Nothing. Get some sleep."

After my mother gave me the mini-tour of the house, I crashed onto her bed. The final thought as my head hit the pillow was that my mother knew I'd killed Eden.

Twenty-four

I drifted in and out of sleep all night, my mind restless from all the excitement of the day but my body exhausted from all the running. Thumping from the furnace coming on jolted me awake all night.

The bedroom door opened and shut a few times during the night. Bleary-eyed, I made out the shape in the room to be my mother. As I drifted off to sleep again, I kept wondering where I was and what was happening that I wasn't in my bed, in my house.

Sometime in the early morning, I started drifting from a sleep state to a more conscious state. Not fully awake yet, I heard the doorbell ring. The front door was below my mother's room. A man's voice shot right up through the window.

"Elizabeth Pierce? We're looking for your daughter, Christa Pierce. Has she been in contact with you? We believe she's in the area."

I sat upright. Thank goodness I had sense enough to ditch Rachel's car, but I left my bag downstairs by the door. As I worked out a way to sneak downstairs to grab my stuff, I saw that it was sitting on a chair in the corner of the room. My mother must have brought everything upstairs while I was asleep.

"Why? What's going on?" My mother's voice shook a little as she spoke.

"We can't say. We have a few questions."

"Is she in some kind of trouble?"

"Again, ma'am, I can't say."

"Can't or won't say?"

"I'm not at liberty to say. If you see or hear from her, call me. Her father is worried about her and would like her home as soon as possible."

"Can't you even give me a hint? She is my daughter, after all."

"Ma'am, I suggest you call your ex-husband and talk with him. He can fill you in on the details. We'll be patrolling the neighborhood. If she's here, you'll have some explaining to do. Have a good day."

Dammit. My father must have been able to talk his way out of the arrest. Or worse. I hit Rachel too hard and she died. Worse still, I didn't hit her hard enough and she lived and was now running her mouth. I had to get out of here. After the front door closed, I heard another voice. It must have been my aunt.

"I told you not to bring her here," she said, sternly.

"What else was I supposed to do?"

"Even after all these years, you're still weak. You were weak for her father and now you're weak for her."

"I failed her once. I can't do it again."

"Don't let your guilt for giving up too soon cloud your judgment. She's a murderer."

"She's my daughter."

"I don't care who she is. I don't want to get in trouble for harboring a criminal."

"She's not involved. She wouldn't do something like that."

"Innocent people don't run, Liz."

"She's scared."

"I'm going to bed. If she's not out of here by the time I wake up, you have to go. I have a good life here. It may not be much, but it's mine, and I worked hard to build it. I'm not going to let anybody ruin it for me, especially that stupid ex-husband of yours and that psycho upstairs." She stomped up the steps and slammed the door.

I scratched my forehead. I had to get out of this house. I'd been an idiot about all of it. Never once did I factor in anybody else but me and my father, and now my mother and aunt were involved.

A knock came at the door. "Come in."

"Ready for breakfast?" My mother's face looked pale, her smile forced. "I can cook a mean omelet, if you're hungry."

"I probably shouldn't have come here." I flung the covers off and reached for my shoes near the bed. "I better get back home." I didn't mean that, of course. What I meant was, I had to get out of here and hide somewhere. Unfortunately, it was late November and it was cold and I had nowhere to run, but I had to do something.

My mother sat on the edge of the bed slowly, eyeing me with that look again, except this time I understood what it meant. "Christa, I'm going to come right out and ask you. Are you somehow involved in the death of your friend?"

I couldn't answer. I couldn't even look her in the eye. "No," I mumbled. "Dad did it."

"Then why did *you* run away?"

"Because... Rachel wouldn't... We got into a fight because she wouldn't let me go. I didn't know what else to do but run."

"By fight you mean an argument?"

"No. I punched her. Hard."

My mother sighed heavily, sadly. "I don't have much money, but we can get a hotel room for a while until you feel better."

"You'd do that for me?"

"I just lied to the police for you."

She studied me, disappointment in her eyes. I was used to that look from my father, Rachel, even Janel, but I never cared. This was like a punch to the gut. "You killed that girl, didn't you?" When I didn't answer right away, she bit her lip and squeezed her eyes shut. Tears rolled down her cheeks. She cupped my face with her hands. "I have to get you out of here."

"How? The police are patrolling the neighborhood."

"My car's in the garage. You can hide in the trunk. If they ask where I'm going, I'll tell 'em I'm going to work. Okay?"

246

I nodded.

"I'll be downstairs making you breakfast. We need to eat before we go. You can take a shower while I get everything together."

While my mother messed around in the kitchen, I went from room to room and looked out the windows for an escape route. I couldn't go out the front windows because it faced the road. Just outside the bathroom window, there was a small roofline that overlooked the backyard. I had no idea where the kitchen was in relation to that window, but it didn't matter.

After I got my things together, I turned on the shower before throwing my bag out onto the roof. Slowly, I tried to go out the window feet first, but it was a tight squeeze, especially for someone my size. I shoved my head out but my broad shoulders got in the way. I put one arm out first and angled my upper body until both shoulders had cleared, all while trying not to make a sound. Nearly slipping on the frozen shingles, I steadied myself, surveying the ground below.

It was a hefty drop to the ground, and I landed hard. Needles of pain shot up my legs. I shook it off and ran.

The town was so small that it wouldn't take long for someone to spot the stranger. I ran on a secondary road for a while, keeping the hoodie up over my face. If I kept at a jogging pace, I'd look like any other jogger in the neighborhood—one who also happened to be wearing a backpack. The thing slowed me down, bouncing off my back with each step, everything inside rattling around. The police would hear me before they saw me.

When I made it to a convenience store, I stopped to catch my breath at the back near a dumpster. I searched through my bag and took out the necessities: coat, money, some snacks, and a bottle of water, and shoved it all in my coat pockets before flinging the backpack in the dumpster. By now, my mother probably realized that was an awfully long shower for one person to take and would have found the bathroom empty, the window open, me gone.

Once I got myself together, I ran, searching for signs for Route 70. Where did I think I was going anyway? Pedestrians weren't allowed to walk on the highway, but I headed in that direction anyway.

I was running at a steady clip when I heard sirens across town. I picked up the pace. The muscles in my legs cramped up, still sore from the night before.

Before long, sirens screeched behind me. I kept running at that steady pace, scanning the neighborhood for ways to get away. I cut through someone's yard and headed in any direction that wasn't where they were.

One of the cops called out my name and told me to freeze. I kept running. The thought of getting taken down by a bullet should have stopped me, but I kept running. Running was my only thought.

Running through the yards was the easy part. I could duck and hide behind sheds, garages, and bushes. So far, no cops had chased me down.

As I crouched behind a row of hedges, I scoped out the next yard over. They had an above-ground swimming pool with a deck. There was a space big enough for me under there. I glanced left and right before sprinting. A dog came out of nowhere and jumped me, knocking me to the ground, jamming my shoulder into a landscaping stone.

"Get off me, you mutt."

He grabbed hold of my arm and wouldn't let go. His teeth cut through my clothes, digging into my skin, the more I struggled to break free from his grip.

Someone whistled for the dog. He ran off toward the back door, wagging his tail. I stumbled to a standing position and kept running. Eyes were on me now. People were peeking out curtains and standing on back porches. In front of me was a privacy fence, and I had nowhere to go but the street. The cops weren't over on that street, so I ran.

I didn't see the cop hiding on the other side of the fence. I also didn't see the arm that clotheslined me right in the throat. I fell backwards. My feet flying in the air was the last thing I saw. My head cracking against the pavement the last thing I heard. Two cops were on top of me, flipping me over and handcuffing me. I didn't fight.

Twenty-five

They chained me to the table like I was a savage animal that would rip them to shreds without the slightest provocation. The cuffs clanged against the table, the chains catching its edge, making me feel like an animal. After the guard locked my chains into place, I kept my hands and arms in front of me, not moving a muscle. They treated me like an animal, yet I didn't act like one.

"You're lucky this state doesn't have a death penalty," the guard mumbled as he double checked the padlocks on my ankles.

"You will refrain from speaking to my client," the lawyer barked back. "Do your job and keep your mouth shut." He was young, probably fresh out of law school, and supplied by the state. My father refused to pay for an attorney for me, and since my mother didn't have the money, I had to get free counsel. I didn't have much confidence in him getting me off by going to trial. My DNA was on my dad's clothes, and since the state was going to try me as an adult, I chose to confess.

I said nothing in response to the guard's comment. I didn't even blink. People wanted me dead. I knew it. I felt it. I heard them say it.

The door clicked open. The district attorney hurried in with Detective Gonzales by his side. "Is there a problem in here?" he asked.

"Tell your man to keep his opinions to himself," my lawyer said.

"Jackson, maybe you should take an early lunch."

"Yes, sir."

Detective Gonzales and the district attorney took their places around the table. The sound of chairs scooting, papers shuffling, and pens clicking filled the small room.

The district attorney cleared his throat and looked at me. "Do you understand what you're doing today?"

I gave a slight nod. "I want to make a full confession."

"All right, you can start any time. State your full name."

"Christa Elizabeth Pierce."

"Look straight ahead at the camera, please, and not at me. Now, what was your relationship to the victim?"

"Eden Rhodes was my best friend."

He waited for me to continue and when I didn't, he said, "And?"

I swallowed hard. "And I killed her."

I told them how my father abused and terrorized me since I was a little girl. How he kept my mother away from me. How he kept her in check with death and rape threats. How he cheated on his wives, including

251

sleeping with some of the students at the university. I told them everything, turning it into a real sob story so they might take sympathy on me and give me a lighter sentence or start looking into my father's activities at the very least. It didn't work.

My father managed to escape any criminal charges, even the attack on my mother. From what I heard, they couldn't track down the guy who attacked her, and since Mom didn't see the guy's face, well, he got away with it. Dad hadn't spoken to me since I was arrested, but not long after I was sent to prison, I got a letter from him. A small part of me had hoped it was a heartfelt apology for failing his only kid. Nope. Seven words. That's it. No, *Dearest Christa* or *Princess* or anything like that.

It said: *No matter what happens, I'll always win.*

For weeks I sat in my cell, seething with anger, that he got away with everything. Until it hit me. He didn't win anything. He may have escaped the law, but he would always be known as the father of a murderer.

But one day, out of nowhere it seemed, all of that changed.

My mother eventually found a full-time teaching job closer to the prison. She promised to visit more often once she got settled, but in between visits, she wrote long letters, keeping me up-to-date on the world outside of these walls.

Through paternity tests, it turned out Kyle Jenkins was the father of Eden's baby and not my dad, like I'd thought.

Rachel eventually recovered from my fist to her face. I offered a flimsy apology, hoping she'd drop the assault charges against me, but all she said was, "Fuck off, psycho." She wasn't as dumb or as weak as I thought, either. She stayed in the marriage because she was playing private investigator, following and recording everything, and everyone, my father did. Once Rachel had enough evidence to build a case against him, she left him. She knew way more than she let on. I underestimated her. The night she found out about Dad and Eden, Rachel took pictures of the long history of texting and sexting between them and saved it as more evidence. She and Dad fought it out in court, and Rachel walked away with a lot of money.

Every week, it seemed, something new and humiliating happened to Dad.

Months went by before my mother finally came to visit. To be honest, I didn't think she ever would, but she came in, apologizing, saying she had been busy setting up house, getting used to working full time again, and dealing with some juicy legal stuff.

"What's going on?" I asked, curious.

"First things first," Mom said, smiling and out of breath. "How are you? You look pale."

"We don't get out much. The food is crap. I miss running. I'm already putting on weight. So, what's all this juicy news?"

"I don't even know where to start." She shook her head and laughed, looking smug. "Uh, let's see. Did you know how old Eden was?"

"My age. Why?"

"You sure?"

I thought about it for a minute. "We always thought she was our age. It never occurred to any of us to ask. But what does that have to do with anything?"

"It makes a big difference to your Dad."

"Still not getting it."

"She was only sixteen. Do you know what that means?"

I shook my head.

"After Eden's funeral, Rachel reached out to Mrs. Rhodes. At first, she didn't want anything to do with Rachel, but after Mrs. Rhodes learned that Eden was messing around with Michael, she changed her mind like that." She snapped her fingers. "Turns out Eden was only sixteen when she was fooling around with your father."

"Oh." I gasped. "Oooohhh."

My mother smiled and nodded. "Mrs. Rhodes filed statutory rape charges against Michael. He tried to deny it, of course."

"He can deny it all he wants, but I heard them going at it in his office. I can offer my testimony if Mrs. Rhodes needs it."

Mom flashed a weak smile and looked away. "I don't think that would be a good idea, hon."

My face grew hot, but I wasn't sure if it was out of anger at the rejection of my offer or embarrassment for Mom pointing it out to me.

"Besides, Eden left a lot of evidence behind. She never erased the texts he sent to her. Some of the stuff he wrote." Mom made a gagging noise and rolled her eyes. "Can't believe I was ever married to that man."

"But what's going to happen to him? Please tell me he's toast."

"Well, once news of the case Mrs. Rhodes and Rachel brought against Michael spread through the community, women and a few young girls came out of the shadows with their own stories. His public image took a huge hit."

"Hold on," I said, interrupting Mom. "Let me savor this." I took in a couple of dramatic breaths. "What else?"

"All those connections he had in the community? They want nothing to do with him now. He lost his job at the college."

Excited, I jumped up from my chair but quickly got reprimanded by the guard. "Sit down."

"Sorry. Just got some good news."

"I don't care. Control yourself."

I shrunk down in the chair and hugged myself to keep my body still. "Sorry, Mom."

She laughed. "You haven't heard the worst of it."

"There's more?"

"Promise me you'll stay calm," she whispered.

I exhaled sharply. "Okay. I'm ready."

"He'll have to register as a sex offender the rest of his life, not to mention jail time if the judge decides."

"Shut. Up." I bit the heel of my hand and bounced my leg. I had been wanting something like this to happen since as long as I could remember.

"You okay?" Mom asked.

"Five minutes," the guard shouted, startling me.

"I'm fine, but if you see Dad, could you tell him something for me?"

"Sure. He has a court appointment in a few weeks. We'll all be there, watching from the gallery. What is it?"

"You know what? Never mind. I'll send a letter."

I said goodbye to Mom and went back to my cell, smiling. Satisfied with all this news about Dad, I wanted to push the knife in deeper, so I wrote the letter. Seven words. That's it.

Who's winning now? Love, your little Princess.

About the author

Laura DiNunno (pronounced: dee-new-no) started writing silly songs for her stuffed animals when she was a kid before moving onto confessional poetry. She writes for all ages, but her first love will always be writing for middle-grade readers (ages 9-12). Her stories usually have some supernatural or psychological element to them. She likes it dark.

She has a B.A. in Theatre. When she's not writing or recording voice over, Laura enjoys listening to music, watching classic movies, snuggling with her two cats, learning to play the piano, and hiking. Her other talents include creative use of colorful language, over-thinking, and being a goofball.

To keep up-to-date on books and such, go to http://lauradinunno.com You can also find her on Instagram @coma_grrl and occasionally on Twitter @comagrrl

www.ingramcontent.com/pod-product-compliance
Lightning Source LLC
Chambersburg PA
CBHW020358210626
46816CB00006BB/2031